THE MISSING NEWLYWEDS

Sergeant Sam Holmes and Doctor Jamie Watson have been given what should be a simple case of finding a couple of newlyweds and their limo driver, who disappeared between their wedding reception venue and hotel. Holmes and Watson are puzzled as to why they would be kidnapped without a ransom being asked. On learning that the bride's deceased first husband was an operative for a large private investigative firm who was killed by a drunk driver, they begin to wonder if the case is not part of a wider conspiracy . . .

Books by Steven Fox
in the Linford Mystery Library:

LEGACIES

STEVEN FOX

THE MISSING NEWLYWEDS

Complete and Unabridged

LINFORD
Leicester

First published in Great Britain

First Linford Edition
published 2018

A catalogue record for this book is available
from the British Library.

ISBN 978–1–4448–3599–1

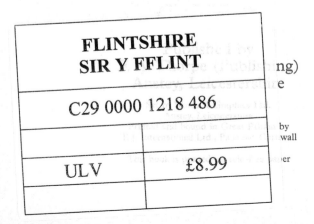

Prologue

(Three Years Ago)

The old rusty clunker was sitting in the parking lot a short distance from the Laun-Dro-Matic. Inside, a man was talking on his cell phone and occasionally taking large swallows from a fifth of bourbon he clutched in his other hand.

'I know what I gotta do!' he vehemently told the other party. 'All of my debts to you will be paid and you don't bother my kin. If you don't keep your end of the bargain, you go down with me.'

The contractor doing repairs on the wooden fence dividing the parking lot from the group of houses behind it watched as the man tossed the phone to the seat beside him and took several pills from a bottle that was in his pocket. He took these with the last of the bourbon in the bottle.

'Time to settle my debts,' he muttered.

The driver started the car and headed east as he floored the accelerator. As he approached the intersection, a pedestrian stepped away from the curb. Hearing the screeching of the tires and seeing the old car approaching him, he jumped back onto the sidewalk.

The driver saw the blue Ford headed his way and veered into the opposing lane. The driver of the Ford had no time to avoid the fiery, fatal collision.

1

(Now)

In an old shack with the windows blacked out and boarded over, two men and one woman were being held for reasons they were not being told. Their captors would not speak and wore long trench coats, gloves, and ski masks to hide their features. When the captives begged to be released or told why they had been abducted, all they got from the masked men was a shake of the head or threatening gestures.

Twice a day their food would be brought in and, one by one, they would have hoods placed over their heads and be escorted to and from the outhouse. A large basin would be filled with water from a ewer. Gestures would tell them to wash their hands and then to eat. The shackles on their ankles were never removed.

'What do want from us?' the woman had once tearfully screamed at the men. 'We're not rich and we don't have any influence for you to exploit! We're just a couple of newlyweds and our limo driver!'

The woman was slapped hard and knocked to the floor. Her husband tried to defend her and was punched in the kidneys. The man who had punched him wagged his finger in a meaningful gesture. They did not attempt to repeat their actions again.

The third man, the limo driver, had been beaten thoroughly and without reason when they had first been kidnapped and had been unable to do more than obey. They did not know that this was part of a plan to soften them up and make them willing to answer questions when the time was right. Nor were they aware that they were being held only a few miles from home.

*　*　*

Samuel Holmes and Jamesina Watson had been certified fit to return to duty just a few days before, after having had received severe knife wounds while investigating the super-Taser affair. They were both glad to be back at their desks and were taking a quick break in the station's break room.

'Your nephew sure was sad to see us get on the plane for home,' Sam said as they sipped their coffees. 'I think that he looks up to you as a second mother, Jamie.'

'He does seem to get excited whenever I visit my brother and his wife,' Jamie commented. 'To tell the truth, I'm gonna really miss him while James and his family are in England.'

'I think your parents are glad that they'll have so much time with their grandson while your brother works on his doctorate,' Sam declared with a thoughtful look. 'Jimmy will be a good detective if he wants to be one when he grows up. The way he notices things and puts them together is truly remarkable for a three-year-old.'

'He loves the way Dad tells stories from Great-great-granddad's journals.'

She started back to the squad room. 'Jimmy really likes you, too, you know. He wanted the doctors to make you well *right now*!'

Sam seemed unusually quiet after they returned to the squad room. She was about to ask him what he was thinking about when Lt. Baker came out of his office.

'Captain Reynolds has a case that he thinks will ease you back into your routine before you get handed a homicide case,' he informed his special team as he placed a folder on their desks. 'As of now, it looks to be a routine missing persons case. However, there are some interesting features.'

They followed the lieutenant into the interview room, where a young couple was waiting. The man was about twenty-five, had medium-length blond hair, was clean-shaven, and neatly but casually dressed in a light blue pullover shirt and freshly pressed jeans. His loafers were made for comfort and well shined. The woman appeared to be two or three years younger and used just a hint of makeup.

Her lemon-colored cotton blouse went well with her navy-blue slacks. Like the man seated beside her, she appeared to take just enough interest in her appearance to look good.

As they entered the room, the man stood up and introduced himself as he held out his hand. 'My name's Fred Jackson and this is my wife, Judy,' he said as Sam took his hand to shake. 'As of three days ago, Judy also became my step-sister.'

'Lt. Baker did tell us that there were interesting features to your case, Mr. Jackson,' Sam said as they sat down. 'Why don't you tell us why you're here?'

'Our parents have both been widowed for a little over three years,' Judy began. 'About nine months ago, my mom and Fred's dad began dating. Soon after that, they decided to get married and were engaged. Three days ago, they were married in a small church ceremony. Fred and I were two of the attendants of honor. The wedding was attended by just a few friends and relatives of the bride and groom. After the reception, they were to be taken to a hotel from where they were to be driven to the airport the next morning to start their honeymoon.'

'But they never arrived?' Jamie's curiosity was beginning to be piqued. 'Where were they last seen?'

'No one has seen them, the limo, or the driver, since they got into the limo to leave for the hotel,' Fred explained. 'In fact, I was standing by the door as the driver held it open for them. They were all smiles and seemed excited to be starting their new life together. They never arrived at the hotel, nor has anything been heard from them or the driver.'

'So nothing seemed unusual?' Sam inquired.

'No,' Judy replied. 'Mom had been talking for the whole week before about their honeymoon plans and how glad she was that she and Mitchell had gotten together after they both had been alone for so long.'

Sam and Jamie jotted down notes and asked questions for the next hour. Fred's and Judy's body language revealed only that they were nervous about being in a police station and that they were both worried about their missing parents.

Lt. Baker, having elderly parents himself, asked the question that was of most concern to him. 'Do either of them have medical or physical problems that need to be addressed quickly? Anything life-threatening if they don't get help soon?'

'Nothing that serious,' Fred said after thinking for a moment. 'Dad takes an iron and vitamin supplement, but that's all that I'm aware of. Does Sally take any prescription medication, Judy?'

'I've never seen anything like that in her medicine cabinet,' she answered.

After Fred and Judy had related everything that they remembered about the wedding and reception, Sam thanked them for their information and told them that they would let them know if they needed to talk to them or had any new information.

After they were gone, Lt. Baker looked at the two detectives and asked, 'Any ideas how you want to proceed?'

'I think we need more information about the limo driver and his company.' Sam looked at his notes. 'The Fair Fare Transportation Service. Low budget and no frills, probably.'

'I'll see what I can find out about their medical histories,' Jamie added. 'They may not have told their children everything.'

'We'll need to have their work histories as well,' Sam commented. 'Perhaps there'll be a clue or two that will surface and give us a motive for the elder Jacksons' disappearance. We have only one side of the triangle: opportunity.'

'Okay, then.' Lt. Baker got up from the table. 'Let's get to work.'

Sam got out his cell phone and dialed information, asking the operator for the number of the limousine company. When he called the number, he received no answer.

'Let's go back to the squad room and check the computer for the address,' Jamie suggested. 'Maybe they just don't care for negative publicity.'

'With the Jacksons only missing for three days?' Sam retorted. 'It's not even on the news services yet.'

'What about R. R.?' Jamie asked. 'I don't like him, but he does get around.'

'I'll take a drive by Fair Fare Transportation and find out if anyone will talk to me. Then we'll both talk with Fred and Judy about the type of work that Mitch and Sally do.'

'While you do that, I'll get started on R. R.' Jamie smiled at the thought of him having to hobble around the city talking to his low-life contacts. The tabloid that he worked for was barely a step above being a yellow journal, but they did occasionally do a well-documented exposé. 'When we talk again to Fred and Judy, let's not forget to ask them for the names of their parents' doctors. I just hope that Fred and Judy are right about their health.'

Their plans for the next few hours made, they agreed to meet at Johanna's later and compare notes.

★ ★ ★

Jamie found R. R. at the park sharing sunflower seeds with the pigeons. 'How's the body healing?' she asked him. R. R. was still recovering from the hit-and-run accident he had suffered when he was helping them with the super-Taser case.

'The docs say things are goin' about as expected.' He looked up as he threw some seeds on the ground. 'You need me to do some undercover research?'

'Who says that I need any research done?'

'And who gave you your first info about the super-Taser and the Golden BBs? You might be able to resist this gorgeous face and perfect bod, but you know that I'm your go-to guy for information.' R. R.'s face lit up with a lecherous grin.

'Sam and I do need you to look into something for us.'

'Anything as dangerous as last time?' he inquired cautiously. 'The Midnight Confessor is still payin' off my hospital bill.'

'Not likely,' Jamie told him. 'Just a couple of newlyweds who disappeared when they left the reception.'

'They didn't just go into hidin' to be alone?'

'Not according to their kids,' she told R. R. and watched his jaw drop in surprise. 'The happy couple had both been widowed for awhile.'

Jamie gave R. R. a quick rundown on what the Jacksons had told her and Sam. Then she asked him to find out anything he could about all four of the Jacksons that wouldn't be on the public info-nets.

'The usual rates?' Again, he grinned at Jamie leeringly.

'You get the exclusive after the case is solved,' Jamie said, 'and my thanks. I believe that's our agreement. Oh, and a small monetary remuneration.'

2

After Sam had located the company's offices, he found a parking space about a block away. The area had once been one of the best districts in the city. It wasn't that bad now, but it had seen its day. The building and its location had confirmed his assessment of it being a low-budget, no-frills type of operation.

When he had opened door, a gentle chime sounded. A middle-aged man in a moderately priced and slightly out of date suit appeared from the back. 'May I help you?' the man graciously offered.

Sam showed him his credentials and asked, 'What can you tell me about the Jackson wedding account? Have you heard anything from your missing driver? Has the vehicle been found?'

'Let's talk in the back,' the manager said. As he passed through the door, he asked a woman to watch the front for a while. The man continued to a cramped but well ordered office at the end of the hall.

'Erickson and his unit haven't been seen since he left the reception,' the man, who had introduced himself as Ryan Jacobs, told Sam. 'Erickson has been with us for several years. He's never had an accident or been given a ticket in all that time. His service record has been excellent and without any major complaints.'

'But there were minor complaints?'

'Some people complained when he refused to violate company rules about the use of intoxicants and other passenger conduct,' Jacobs told Sam. 'Nothing that would get him or the company into trouble.'

'So,' Sam inquired, 'he's never given you, or your company, any trouble or cause for concern previously?'

'We've never had a situation like *this* before,' was Mr. Jacobs's reply. 'I do hope nothing serious has befallen Erickson or his party.'

'What was the itinerary?' Sam asked. 'Were there supposed to be any special stops between the reception and the hotel? Perhaps a place that had a special meaning for the couple?'

'Not that Erickson had mentioned over the radio,' Mr. Jacobs answered. 'His last report just said that he had picked up his clients and was taking them to their hotel. He was scheduled to pick them up early the following morning and deliver them to the airport.'

★ ★ ★

Sam looked at Jamie after they had told each other of their day's activities and frowned. 'Mr. Jacobs didn't appear to be worried, but I sensed he was actually a more than a little concerned,' he told her.

'What makes you think that?'

'His voice and his body language seemed to be telling me two different things.' Sam's frown deepened as he reviewed the conversation with Jacobs in his mind. 'He kept looking around the office as if he was expecting to see someone, but his other body signals showed a kind of calmness that I thought was unusual. His eyes and voice gave it the lie.'

'Not the way you'd expect someone with a missing and apparently valued employee to react, was it?'

'No.' Sam shook his head. 'More like someone under a lot of stress.'

Sam and Jamie agreed to meet at his house for breakfast the next morning and then go to Fred and Judy's place. Although they were certain that the young couple would be home as it was the weekend, they agreed to call and make an appointment before they left Johanna's.

The couple lived in an older set of apartments in the moderately priced southwest section of the city. The apartment complex, while beginning to show its age, exhibited signs of having been renovated perhaps within the last decade.

'It looks like the Jacksons are trying stay within a budget,' Sam remarked as they drove into a convenient parking space. 'If they're sticking to a plan, they are being more fiscally responsible than most young people nowadays.'

'I think that may tell us a thing or two about their folks, too,' Jamie added. 'Mitchell and Sally probably have set the example for them.'

The door was answered quickly and Sam and Jamie were invited in by a slightly nervous Fred Jackson. 'Judy will be back shortly,' he told them as he showed them into the sparsely furnished living room. 'Judy realized we're almost out of several items for Sunday dinner. She enjoys getting fancy on weekends.'

Everyone had just gotten comfortable when they heard Judy's voice from the doorway. 'Fred,' she asked as she put a bag of groceries on the kitchen table, 'have our guests been waiting long? I tried to be done as quickly as possible, but the store only had two check stands open.'

'That's all right,' Jamie said as she went to help Judy put away the things from the store. 'We only just arrived. Sam, why don't you and Fred do some male bonding while I help Judy put things away?'

Fred and Sam walked out onto the

patio. 'I know it's still early to be asking,' Fred said as he pulled out a pack of gum and put a stick in his mouth, 'but has anything new been heard from Dad or Sally?'

'Nothing really.' Sam looked over the well-kept lawns and other greenery. 'Perhaps you could tell us what Mitchell and Sally do for a living. Maybe Dr. Watson and I could find a connection to their disappearance.'

'Well . . . ' Fred's voice and manner showed only a slight reluctance to speak. ' . . . until Mom lost her battle with cancer, Dad worked for a large medical supply company. He took early retirement after she passed away. Mom's medical bills were nearly all covered by the catastrophic illness rider on her medical insurance. Her life insurance policy paid the rest of the bills, so Dad's pension allowed him to live without having to worry about his finances. He volunteers for a couple of days a week at the local senior center, and that's helped him work through his grieving period.

'Judy's mom works out of her home

making children's blankets and clothes. Several years ago Sally had gotten a seller's license, and Judy's dad had helped turn the garage into a shop. Judy told me that Sally was devastated when she lost her husband in an auto accident caused by a drunk driver. The settlement and the accidental death benefits from Tom's company helped Sally get through the early financial difficulties until she was ready to open her shop full-time again.'

'Did your families know each other well before you and Judy were married?'

'No,' Fred replied. 'Judy and I had met less than a year after she lost her dad and I lost my mom. Judy had just started college and I was a junior. When Judy and I decided to get married, Dad and Sally were quickly becoming friends. I would like to think that seeing us together is what decided them to take a chance at love the second time around.'

'Have they made any decisions about living arrangements after the wedding?' Sam probed. 'Were they planning on selling or renting one or both of the houses?'

'There had been some talk of selling or renting Dad's house and keeping Sally's home since the shop was well established. Dad has even offered to allow me and Judy to take over the payments on his house instead of continuing to rent this apartment. Judy and I would love to do it and we *could* afford the payments, but we haven't decided yet.'

★ ★ ★

Jamie chatted with Judy as they put everything into their proper storage spaces. 'So,' she asked Judy, 'how did you meet Fred? Had you known him long before you got married?'

Judy told Jamie about how she and Fred had met in a study group when she had first started going to the university, how their mutual loss of a parent had begun their relationship, and how it had blossomed into the romance that eventually led to marriage.

'How about your mom and Fred's dad? How did they meet?'

'I think it was at a gathering for the

21

parents to get to know the friends of their children and some of the other parents. By that time Fred and I had been dating for some time. Both of our parents were just getting adjusted to widowhood and they were still very lonely.'

'What interests do they have in common?' Jamie inquired. 'What do they like to do together?'

'Mitch helps Mom run her shop at home when he isn't down at the Senior Center doing volunteer work. He had taken early retirement after Fred's mom passed away. Once or twice a month, one of the neighbors who helps keep the shop running smoothly will take over so she and Mitch can work together at the Senior Center and spend the day together. Sometimes they'll spend an evening together at a dance club or at the theater. They often have dinner out together. Neither Fred nor I were surprised when they told us they were getting married.'

'How did the two of you feel about becoming step-siblings?'

'A little awkward at first, I suppose,'

Judy remarked after a moment's contemplation. 'Mitch and Mom are good for each other, and we can both tell that they're happy not to spend their golden years alone.'

'And Fred seems to feel the same way?' Jamie quizzed. 'He doesn't feel that Sally is interfering with his relationship with his father?'

'If he does,' Judy nearly laughed, 'he's better at hiding his feelings than I've been able to credit him with!'

3

'If we're to believe the younger Jacksons,' Sam mused as they drove back to the station, 'then each of them is happy for their parents, even though there was some awkwardness at first with their own new relationship.'

'That would, I think,' responded his partner, 'accurately state what we've learned. Did you get the name of the company that Mitch worked for before his early retirement?'

'The Medical Supply Superstore,' Sam told her. 'It's a multi-state limited liability company based up in Sacramento. They distribute all sorts of medical hardware and pharmaceuticals to hospitals, medical supply houses, and prescription drug outlets throughout the country. They have sales that equal several billion dollars at wholesale a year. That adds up to millions of dollars profit over the cost of production.'

'Depending on how high an echelon he was on,' Jamie observed, 'and his length of service, his pension could range from 'more than adequate' to 'highly substantial'.'

'And if the medical and life insurance policies paid off all of the medical bills,' Sam told her, 'his fiscal position could be such that, if he were even the least bit frugal, he could live quite comfortably and still put money away in a contingency fund. What did you find out about Judy's mom and dad?'

'Judy's dad was an operative for a nationwide private investigation and security company,' was Jamie's reply. 'His death was investigated by his company and some fairly high-level law enforcement groups. The driver of the other vehicle was also killed in the accident. A blood alcohol check during the autopsy showed that the other driver had twice the legal limit of alcohol in his bloodstream, mixed with an over-the-counter cold remedy medicine. The other driver was determined to be driving under the influence, so Tom's company insurance policy paid a huge indemnity to Sally. That, and her husband's life and personal accident insurance, allowed her some grief-time without having to keep her shop open full time. Also, the mortgage lacked only a few payments before being paid off.'

Sam asked the name of the investigation company and told Jamie that he would check for the case that Sally's late husband was working on at the time of his death. Jamie offered to find out what position Mitchell Jackson had held before his early retirement.

'We don't know if this is a kidnapping yet.' She was intrigued at the mystery behind the newlyweds' disappearance. 'Or if some as yet undiscovered accident was the cause.'

'An accident hasn't been ruled out,' Sam agreed, 'but neither has foul play. Vengeance and/or vendetta could be as likely at this point as kidnapping for extortion. Fred mentioned that Mitch's house still has a mortgage. Let's find the name of the lender and see what we can find out about the disposition of the loan.

Until we know more about the Jacksons, elder and younger, everything needs to be investigated.'

★　★　★

Sam and Jamie returned to the station to write up their notes in report form and to check their computers for accident reports and for news of any ransom demands, threats against Mitchell and Sally Jackson, or claims of responsibility for their disappearance.

'No joy in Mudville, Sergeant, Doctor?' Lt. Baker said as he joined them at their desks.

'So far — ' Jamie looked up from her computer screen. ' — it looks as if Casey has struck out.'

'We still have several innings to play, though,' Sam quipped. 'The game has just begun.'

'Tell me what you have so far,' Lt. Baker requested. 'Let's see if anything comes to light.'

Sam and Jamie printed out their reports and took them into the lieutenant's office.

After Baker had read through them, he questioned them on their plans for follow-ups. When they had apprised him of the directions they wished to go, he offered to check into the duties of Sally Jackson's deceased husband at the time of his death.

'Sometimes a married investigator will bounce ideas off his or her spouse. Of course without breaking confidentiality rules,' he said thoughtfully. 'Sally may not have known anything specific, but perhaps his enemies didn't know that. The wedding may have been their best opportunity to find out what she knows. American Investigations may be more willing to talk with a lieutenant than a sergeant. If not, perhaps Capt. Reynolds can persuade them to part with the information we need.' He paused and then added: 'Checking with the local offices of the Medical Supply Superstore is a sound idea. Someone may have had a beef with the way their account was handled. It may have just taken this long to find out who the person was that they feel is responsible.'

The two detectives thanked their

superior for his assistance and left the office.

'This case may turn out to be more difficult that the surface indicates,' Lt. Baker mused as he called Capt. Reynolds with an update on the case.

4

After making an appointment with the district manager of the Medical Supply Superstore, Sam and Jamie decided to stop by the offices of the Midnight Confessor to see if R. R. was in.

'He said he was going over to the corner where he was run down the last time he got involved with you two,' they were told by one of R. R.'s fellow reporters. 'Said he wanted to see the place where it happened.'

'We know the place,' Jamie replied, and then asked, 'How long ago did he leave?'

'He left about ten minutes ago. On foot,' was the answer.

Jamie drove while Sam kept a lookout for R. R.

'We don't want to startle him,' Sam told her. 'When we spot him, honk the horn before you pull beside him at the curb. It'll let him know that it's us.'

About a block from the corner where

R. R. had been struck down by a hit-and-run driver, Sam saw their quarry. 'There he is.' Sam pointed at R. R. 'Let him know we're here and find a place where we can pick him up or let me out.'

Jamie did as she was asked as R. R. stopped and waited for her to pull up beside him. When she had stopped, Sam opened the back passenger door and invited R. R. in.

'Looks like everyone's back on the job,' he said as he slid into the back seat. 'I hear you had a fairly rough time over there in England, Sam.'

'Nearly as bad you had here,' Sam responded. 'Heard any news on our missing newlyweds?'

'Nada. Zip. Zero! The only thing I know is that it's been nearly twice as long as good news is usually hoped for.'

'Do you know anything about the former Sally Jenkins' children's blanket and clothing shop on Gemson Avenue?' Jamie inquired.

'Small place,' R. R. told her after thinking for several heartbeats. 'Been in

31

operation about ten years. Makes a modest profit.'

'The owner is one of our missing persons,' Sam reported. 'What do you know about her?'

'Just that her husband, Tom, was killed in a vehicle accident caused by a drunk driver.'

'Nothing else?'

'Just a gut feelin'.' There was a long pause.

'Okay, R. R., give,' Sam ordered.

'Tom worked for some agency that found out things,' R. R. said as he squirmed in his seat. 'This news is about three years old and, to me, the cops' report don't exactly say that two plus two equals four.'

'How so?'

'You remember how my 'accident' was no accident?'

'What has that to do with Tom Jenkins?'

'Just that if I'd been in a car, it mighta been passed off as a drunk driver, too.'

'Are you talking about dirty cops, R. R.?' Jamie asked.

'Mebbe, mebbe not.' R. R. shrugged

his shoulders dismissively. 'But mebbe the evidence was tainted beforehand.'

'How?' Jamie asked, incensed.

'I don't know,' was the reply. 'Remote control. Or perhaps the guy didn't get liquored up until he knew his target was near and downed a fifth of somethin' in a hurry, then purposely plowed into Jenkins's car.'

'Sort of like a suicide bomber?' Sam questioned.

'With the right incentive,' Jamie said thoughtfully, 'anything is possible.'

'Let's hope that the lieutenant or the captain can find out what Tom Jenkins was working on when he died,' Sam said.

'We still have to find out if there's a connection between Tom, Sally, and her new husband,' Jamie mused. 'Where do you want us to drop you off, R. R.?'

'Are you kiddin' me, Dr. Watson?' R. R. snorted at his hosts. 'This could get interestin'.'

'Remember that you almost became a crispy critter,' Sam reminded him, 'and then someone tried to turn you into road kill.'

'And don't forget the nameless body dropped on your editor's doorstep,' Jamie added.

'Goes with the territory,' R. R. told her.

★ ★ ★

Jamie drove to downtown and found a parking space near the Medical Supply Superstore's office and showroom at Roosevelt and Taft. Sam, Jamie, and R. R. were greeted by a man in an expensively tailored three-piece suit, silk tie, and Italian leather dress loafers. Sam told the man that they had an appointment and showed his badge and credentials. He asked if there was anyone on duty who could supply answers to some questions about a former employee.

'Perhaps Mr. Zeiter, the district, would be authorized,' the man said as he went to a desk phone and dialed a three-digit number. After short conversation of words made up mostly of one or two syllables, they were shown to the office of Mr. Zeiter.

'What can I do for you, Detectives?'

said the man behind the desk, who was even more richly dressed. 'I have limits on what I can repeat about our employees, past or present.'

'As far as we know,' Jamie volunteered, 'Mitchell Jackson has done nothing wrong. He and his new bride went missing, along with their limousine and chauffeur just after they left the reception party. We're hoping to find out what happened.'

'You mean the man whose wife died about three years ago?'

'That's right,' Sam responded. 'Could you tell us what kind of employee he was and what his responsibilities were? What did he do for your company?'

'He was one of our best customer relations managers,' Mr. Zeiter related to them. 'When his wife passed away after a long illness, we offered to let him take a leave of absence for up to a year at three quarters pay as bereavement time. After a couple of months, on his thirty-fifth anniversary with the company, he decided to take an early retirement. He was only fifty-eight at the time, if I remember correctly. He kept his full medical benefits and was given a pension of $60,000 a year until he turns seventy-five. That doesn't include a cost-of-living adjustment calculated every two years.'

'That sounds fairly generous,' Jamie commented.

'If he had stayed until he was sixty-five, he would have earned another fifteen thousand per year, plus an adjustment every year.'

'Did he have any life insurance from the company?' Sam was a bit surprised at the size of Mitch's retirement benefits. 'Did he have an IRA account or a 401k plan account?'

'He had his own life insurance policy, and you'd have to talk to his financial adviser about his investments.'

'One more question, Mr. Zeiter,' Jamie said. 'How did he get along with his fellow workers? Did he have any close friends, or anyone with whom he couldn't get along?'

'Until his wife took ill, he had no trouble with the others. After that, he was often withdrawn and sometimes grouchy.

It was a very bad year for him, emotionally. Most people who knew about his wife were understanding and just backed away when he was having a particularly bad day.'

'And how did that affect his work?' Sam inquired.

'When he was working with a customer, he seemed to be his old self. Helpful, positive. A problem-solver.'

'Thank you for your time, Mr. Zeiter.' Sam, Jamie, and R. R. shook Mr. Zeiter's hand as they prepared to leave.

As they walked out of the office, Mr. Zeiter told them that if they needed any more information, they were welcome to return. Jamie handed Mr. Zeiter a card with their names and contact numbers on it. 'Call us if you remember anything that could help us in our search,' she said as they walked to the exit.

5

Jamie dropped R. R. off at his paper's office and then she and Sam returned to the police station. Sam switched on his computer and checked the online version of the paper, looking for the article about the death of Tom Jenkins. When he found it, he checked the date.

'May first, three years ago,' he muttered to himself.

'What was that, Sam?' Jamie said from her desk.

'What? Oh!' He looked up from the screen that he was reading. 'Just talking to myself. Tom Jenkins was killed on May first three years ago. It just seems a little odd for Sally to remarry only a month before the anniversary of her husband's death.

'This report states that the vehicle that caused the accident headed straight into Jenkins' car. The blood alcohol level was a surprise at the autopsy. The eye-witness reports all claimed that the vehicle appeared to purposely run straight into Jenkins. There was no attempt to change course, and Jenkins had little or no time to react and avoid a collision.'

'R. R.'s gut feeling may be right about Jenkins's death,' Jamie said when Sam finished the report in the newspaper. 'What about the police report on the accident? And the coroner's report?'

'I'll look those up while you check with the lieutenant about what he found out about Tom's background and what he was working on at the time of his death.'

* * *

After checking in with his editor and relating what he had learned during his time with Sam and Jamie, R. R. checked the online morgue of the *LonCal Times* for information about Tom Jenkins's death.

Hmm, he thought to himself as he read the detailed news report. *There's just enough here to make me doubt the total accuracy of the whole situation. I wonder if there's still enough talk on the street for 'Johnny Oh' to pick up on?*

R. R. changed out of his wrinkled suit and into the rags and griminess of his persona of Johnny Oh, street person and information broker. He also signed out for some petty cash to lubricate wagging tongues. When he was all set, he walked out the back door and into the alley behind the newspaper office. Having made sure that he hadn't been seen leaving, he worked his way across town to the street corners occupied by derelicts, prostitutes, drug dealers, and gang bangers.

'Hey Johnny!' said a voice from a doorway near a trash-filled alley. 'Ain't seen you around in a while. What's your thing, man?'

'Just a little o' this, a little o' that,' Johnny Oh responded. 'What's goin' down, Slash?'

'Same as always,' Slash told him. 'If you're back to work the 'hood, you gotta pay Maxie for the privilege now.'

'When did Maxie get to be the high muckety-muck?'

''Bout six weeks ago,' Slash informed him. 'He and Stonewall had a disagreement. Maxie won the argument.'

Johnny Oh's got to be seen more often, R. R. thought to himself. *I'm out of touch with this 'hood. And that ain't good.* 'Got hit by a car,' 'Johnny' informed Slash. 'Been outta the loop for a while. I'll pay my respects to Maxie first thing now that I know.'

'I'm shore Maxie'll be glad to see you, Johnny.' Slash grinned as he disappeared into the dark doorway. 'You always came through with the goods for Stonewall.'

★ ★ ★

After an hour of walking the street of Maxie's — formerly Stonewall's — neighborhood, Johnny Oh found someone who remembered the accident on Tenth Avenue three years ago.

'Yeah,' the rummy said after accepting the offered five-dollar bill, 'I oughta 'member! I was at the corner waitin' for the light. This guy come gunnin' 'cross the street like the devil's demons was after 'im just as a blue Ford was comin' from the opposite direction, not expectin' nothin'. The other guy, drivin' an old Junker of sum kind, veers onta the Ford's side o' the road and head-ons 'im. Musta been doin' sixty, seventy miles an hour. I just barely got outta the way.'

'The cops talk to you, Jerry?' Johnny pulled out a bottle of cheap alcohol in a brown paper bag from his coat pocket. Jerry eyed the bottle as if it was a long-lost lover, returned at last.

'They wanted to, but I needed stitches, so off to the hospital I goes,' reported Jerry with a wink. 'Nat'rally, I sneaks outta there when the docs' backs are turned after they're through with me. No one axed me 'bout it 'til now.'

'Thanks, Jerry,' Johnny Oh said as he gave him the bottle.

As Johnny Oh left Jerry the Rummy, he pretended not to notice the high-end coupé that followed him. *Probably some of Maxie's soldiers checkin' me out*, he thought. *Might as well meet Maxie now as later.*

Just as Johnny was about to cross at the

corner, the coupé turned in front of him. The door opened and a big, muscular and mean-looking man in an Italian suit and tie with Amerindian features got out. 'Get in,' he instructed Johnny as he leaned the seat-back forward to allow him into the back seat. 'Maxie will be lookin' forward to making your acquaintance.'

'Been wonderin' when the man would invite me over for a chat,' Johnny quipped as he slipped into the back and the coupé headed toward the southern city limits.

6

R. R. was driven to a miniature hotel that had been converted into a luxury single-family home about half a mile inside the city limits.

'I didn't know homes like this existed south of the King and Queen Avenues.' R. R. gave a low, appreciative whistle as the luxury coupé stopped at the front door.

'One of the perks Maxie got in the settlement with Stonewall,' the big Amerindian told him as he got out to give R. R. room to exit. 'The butler'll take you to Maxie's study.'

At the door, a man in a traditional butler's tuxedo took R. R.'s hat and jacket. 'Follow me.' The butler headed down a wide hallway after hanging up R. R.'s outer apparel. 'Mr. Maxie is expecting you.'

At the open doorway to a large study, R. R. saw a large mahogany desk with an ergonomic high-backed chair. As the chair slowly turned around to face him, R. R. saw a well-dressed black American of middle age with a slightly overweight but well-built physique sitting there, a cigar in his hand.

'Greetings, Johnny,' a deep, cultured baritone voice said. 'I'm Maxie Stonn. Please, sit down.' Maxie gestured to one of the two seats in front of the desk. 'I've been told that you are in the information brokerage business. Are you looking to buy, or sell? Either way, you have to pay me a percentage, unless I commission you to find out something for me. Then I'll pay you what it's worth to me, as agreed to beforehand.'

'And if I don't agree, or can't find out what you want?' Johnny wanted to know exactly where he stood with Maxie before he agreed to anything. It could keep him out of trouble later. 'What happens then?'

'If we can't come to an agreement between gentlemen,' Maxie grinned, 'then you don't leave the Southside the next time you come within my reach. If you don't find what I want, but you make your best effort, I may have you roughed up as a reminder that I don't like failure.'

'Stonewall asked for a ten percent cut of what I was paid, and I also had to pay him a flat rate of $100 per piece o' info that I learned on my own. What's your offer?'

'Stonewall's agreement sounds fair,' Maxie said after he inhaled a lungful of cigar smoke and let it out. 'What are you seeking now? I know that you've been asking questions.'

'A couple o' friends o' mine want me to find out what I can 'bout a couple that vanished on their weddin' night. They think it mighta been foul play.' Johnny crossed his legs and appeared to relax in his chair. 'No one's seen them, the chauffeur, or the car since they left the reception for the hotel. My friends think that mebbe their deceased former spouses had enemies that have been takin' their time for revenge. Oh, yeah, here's a real beaut. Their kids are married ta each other.'

'That's a real belly laugh, all right,' Maxie said. 'If I or my boys find out anything, you pay me $50 for each bit of news and you can keep all of what you get from your client. Sound reasonable?'

'Quite reasonable.'

'Jeffords will show you to the door. Sam and Dick will take you back to where they picked you up.'

★　★　★

When Sam and Jamie returned to the department, they were intercepted by Lt. Baker. 'Got some news for you,' he informed them. 'Come into my office and we'll talk.'

After everyone was seated, Baker placed a file folder on his desk. 'American Investigations faxed a copy of the reports that Tom Jenkins made during his last case.'

Sam pulled the folder toward him and Jamie.

'This looks like a fairly routine investigation into suspected industrial espionage,' Jamie commented after she and Sam had quickly scanned the file's contents. 'Someone may not have wanted the investigation to go forward because there was dirt being swept under the rug.'

'What did their investigation conclude about the accident?' Sam inquired, thinking about what R. R. had told them. 'Could the 'accident' have been a cover-up for murder?'

'The team from traffic accidents and control wondered about that, too.' Lt. Baker frowned as he pulled out two more folders from his desk drawer. 'Both our team and the team from American Investigations felt that the evidence was inconclusive, but leaned toward a traffic accident caused by a case of DUI.

'While the blood alcohol level was twice the legal limit, the coroner believed that the intake may have been too soon to have been debilitating. He said that the distribution of alcohol in the bloodstream wasn't what he would have expected for such a high level. He estimated that a large quantity may have been ingested probably not more than ten minutes before the accident. He also said that time estimates were far from being an exact science. Both teams accepted his conclusions.'

'So,' Jamie sighed, 'the final report is still in doubt. How would a change from death caused by an intoxicated driver to willful murder/suicide affect Sally Jackson's settlement?'

'I'm not sure,' her superior told her, 'but after three years, I don't believe that the insurance company that paid the settlement is likely to get a reimbursement worth the expense.'

7

Before Jamie and Sam left for the day, they made arrangements with Mitch Jackson's mortgage lender for an interview the next afternoon. They also agreed to meet at Johanna's to unwind and informally discuss what they knew about the case. They both felt that the chance of finding Mitch and Sally in reasonable health was remote and getting more unlikely by the hour.

Half an hour after Sam and Jamie had been seated in their usual booth, a grimy but slightly familiar man walked in. One of the bouncers intercepted him while he was still in the foyer. Johanna joined the two men as they began a firm but quiet discussion.

'Sir,' the bouncer was saying to the apparent vagrant, 'we do have minimum standards of dress. And, as we reserve the right to refuse service to anyone, I must ask that you leave.'

'I'm working undercover for Sgt. Holmes and Dr. Watson,' the vagrant replied. 'If you'll just give them my card, I'm sure they'll want to see me.'

Johanna took the proffered card. When she read it, she left the vagrant and the bouncer in the foyer and went to Sam and Jamie's booth.

'This person has a business card from a man that all three of us know. But he doesn't look like him. Do you want to see him, or shall I have him escorted out?'

'He's scum of the earth,' Jamie sneered. 'Show him the sidewalk. We'll deal with him in five minutes. Outside.'

Johanna nodded to the bouncer, who had been waiting for a sign from her as to his next move. He approached his boss and asked, 'Yes ma'am? Show him the door?'

'Yes,' Johanna answered, 'but make sure the sergeant and good doctor get to speak with him outside undisturbed. They have a few questions for him.'

The bouncer roughly took the vagrant's arm and unceremoniously took him out of the door, shoving him outside. 'Stay here until you're told to leave,' he ordered. 'I'll be watching. Remember, this place is full of cops. You can be bird-cage liner before you get two blocks. Be grateful that you get to have your interview.'

Jamie and Sam walked out and began to look up and down the street. When they were each satisfied that their little show was convincing, Sam asked, 'Who are you supposed to be, R. R.? Can't tell the players without a cast list.'

'Name's Johnny Oh,' R. R. told them. 'Someone I get info from now and then. I may have news, but I'm not sure how reliable it is, nor how recent.'

'Tell us what you have, Johnny,' Jamie encouraged. 'We'll check it out and tell you if we need you to follow up.'

'Before you do,' Sam said, 'take a swing at me. And I do mean make it look good. We may need Johnny's reputation intact for later.'

Without warning, Johnny 'R. R.' Oh yelled, 'You damn liars! You said you'd give me a hundred bucks for what I just told you. Now you don't wanna give with the dough?' Then he took a roundhouse swing that would have broken Sam's nose if he hadn't taken a step back.

While Johnny was off balance, Sam had pulled both of Johnny's arms behind him and handcuffed him before he could recover.

'Assaulting a peace officer will get you a nice vacation at the crossbar hotel, Johnny,' Sam growled. He turned to Jamie. 'Call for a pick-up. Our friend needs to cool off for a while.'

Jamie called Lt. Baker's cell phone number and explained that they had an unruly informant. Using her personal code words, she made the lieutenant aware that the trip to the police station was for show and that they would need a secure interview room.

In a few minutes, a police cruiser stopped in front of Johanna's and R. R. was taken to the station. Sam and Jamie went back inside to pay their bill. As they were leaving, Jamie gave Johanna a wink and a nod to let her know that everything was under control and that they would explain later.

When Sam and Jamie reached the station, R. R. and Lt. Baker were waiting in the interview room. 'I think that act outside of Johanna's will keep people satisfied that you may have been scammed by us,' Sam said as he sat down. 'Now tell us what Johnny found out.'

R. R. told them about meeting Slash, what Jerry the Rummy had told him, and about his run-in with Maxie Stonn.

'Slash told me that Maxie had taken over from Stonewall about six weeks ago,' he reported. 'That woulda been 'round the time I was laid up. I was expectin' Maxie's boys to show up, so when they grabbed me I wasn't surprised. Maxie's got a real nice place near the city's southern border.'

'We knew that Stonewall had been replaced,' Lt. Baker remarked. 'Nice to know by who. We'll be keeping an eye on Mr. Stonn. Thanks, R. R.'

'If Jerry doesn't believe Tom Jenkins's death was an accident, why didn't he come forward before now?' Jamie inquired. 'Tell us what 'Johnny' found out.'

R. R. told them about Jerry the

Rummy being at the corner three years ago and what he had seen. 'Being a street person,' R. R. said, 'he has a natural distrust of authority figures. At his first chance he disappeared, not wanting to complicate his life with a police interview.

'When I, as Johnny Oh, street person and information broker, offered five dollars for information on a three-year-old traffic death, Jerry was the only one to come forward. When I asked him about bein' questioned, he said the paramedics took him to the hospital for stitches. As soon as their backs were turned after they finished with him, he left and never talked to anyone before now. While we were talkin', I let him see the bottle of booze I had. After he told me all that he remembered, I gave it to him. About half a block away, I spotted an expensive coupé followin' me. I figured it was some of Maxie's boys, so I played dumb. The rest you've already heard.'

'Okay, 'Johnny'.' Lt. Baker stood up to stretch his back. 'You're going to be our guest for another hour or two. Then you'll be let go and the charges dropped. Your buddies south of the Kings and Queens should believe that you got rousted.'

★ ★ ★

Later, when Sam and Jamie returned to their booth at Johanna's, Johanna joined them. 'Which one of you kids want to explain what happened?' she asked as she sat down. 'This can't happen again, okay? It's bad for business and the reputation of my place.'

'We had to protect 'Johnny Oh's' reputation,' Sam explained. 'We may not care for his tabloid writing or his personality, but R. R. does know how to dig up dirt on certain people in this city that can be useful to us when we go after bad guys who appear to be good guys. Johnny Oh is one of his sources.'

'We'll have Johnny use R. R. to get his messages to us from now on,' Jamie offered.

'As long as there's no more scenes like the last one on my doorstep,' Johanna sighed. 'This is a family place as well as a cop shop. Keep it as low-key as you can.

56

That's all I ask of any of you law hunks.'

Johanna got up from their table to meet and greet her other customers. Before she walked away, she whispered, 'Watch your backs.'

'Always,' they said in unison.

8

In a rundown shack not far from Rosita's Cantina on the east side of the city, two upper-middle-aged adults in disheveled wedding clothes and a third in a dirty chauffeur's uniform were each chained at their ankles.

'Why are they doing this, Mitch?' the fiftyish woman in a blue bridal dress asked plaintively. 'What do they want?'

'I don't know what they want, Sally,' answered the older man, wearing a wrinkled tuxedo. 'They haven't said one word to us since we were grabbed. How are you doing, Mr. Erickson? They roughed you up pretty badly when we were pulled out of the car.'

The chauffeur looked out from blackened and swollen eyes. 'I been better,' he answered through his puffy lips and bruised jaw. 'I seen pictures of POWs after the V. C. 'questioned' 'em. This ain't nothin' compared to what they went through.'

'What's your opinion about this horrible thing, Mr. Erickson?' Sally, who had obviously cried herself out, asked. 'Do you have any ideas why they've chosen us?'

'Other than they did it 'cause they could,' Erickson painfully replied, 'I have no idea. When they bumped the limo was the first I suspected it was more'n just a regular traffic accident, ma'am. They really put a fright into me when they pulled me outta the vehicle and began to beat me up.'

'Do you think they're looking for a ransom?' Mitch continued. 'Could the limo have given them ideas as to our financial status?'

'With these punks nowadays — ' Erickson looked at Mitch, attempting to answer without frightening Sally. ' — who knows. They get the idea that somethin' might be fun, and they do it without another thought.'

The three prisoners went silent as they heard the crunch of tires on the gravel surrounding the shack. Car doors slammed and they soon heard the key turn in the lock. The door opened and two men wearing ski masks and long leather trench coats came in carrying bags of fast food. The men placed their burdens on the table in the front room. After their trip outside, a gesture was made that said, 'Here's your food. Eat.' Then they went back outside and locked the door.

After Sally, Mitch and Erickson heard the car leave, Erickson looked at the others and remarked, 'Whatever their plans are, they don't mean for us to starve. I believe they've fed us enough to fill up on twice a day ever since we been here. We might as well eat while they let us.'

'You don't think we should keep something back?' Sally asked, fear in her eyes. 'Just in case they change their minds?'

'No,' her new husband told her calmly. 'The food is too perishable to try to hoard. What we need to do is plan how we can escape and not get recaptured.

Once we've done that, and we know where we are, we can let the authorities or our families know what's become of us and where to find us. Fred and Judy surely have the police looking for us.'

'My boss at least has someone lookin' for the limo,' Erickson commented. 'He's only got three vehicles, and one o' them is always down for routine maintenance. With one o' them missin', he's losin' half his business and pushin' the red zone.'

Sally seemed to perk up at this news. 'So there's hope that we'll be rescued?'

'As long as we're alive, there's always hope,' Mitch answered his bride, 'but our chances will improve if we can figure a way to help ourselves.'

'The ankle chains and the locked door are the biggest problems we gotta solve.' Erickson hobbled over to the door. 'This lock don't look too hard to bypass. If we can get the hobbles off of us, I think I can get us outta here. After that it's just decidin' when to go and findin' out where we are. We can find a phone or flag someone down then.'

'With the schedule that they've been

keeping,' Mitch responded, 'we may have as much as twelve hours to get away if we wait until after they bring our food the next time. I think that after we get the food would be our best chance to get away without being seen. Do you have a guess as to where we might be, Mr. Erickson? You know this city pretty well I would assume from your occupation.'

'Just that we're probably somewhere toward the east side. The sounds from the road made me think that we were headed toward the desert away from the main roads. Other things, like the turns we made, felt right for our direction, too. The time it took us to get here tells me we're way out, probably near the city limits.'

'That's good to know.' Mitch was glad to see that Erickson had been so observant, even after having been beaten by their captors. 'When we get out, we can use the stars at night to get our bearings. The first Persian Gulf War taught me a lot about night navigation.'

With renewed hope and the beginnings of a plan, they set about finding a way of getting themselves free from their shack-les.

* * *

With a city map in front of them, Sam and Jamie tried to figure where the Jacksons and their driver could be hidden.

'On the east side, the area around Rosita's looks like our people could be held there if they're still alive,' Sam surmised. 'There are plenty of abandoned shacks and old mine shafts out there. They might even be there if they aren't alive. Plenty of places to hide three bodies and a limo.'

'That's probably the best place to look,' Jamie agreed. 'Dr. Conner has me on rotation for autopsies tonight and tomorrow night. Perhaps R. R. would like to go with you tonight.'

'Even if he doesn't, I think that I can put him in the proper frame of mind,' Sam said with a malicious grin. 'We already have him on the hook. All we have to do is reel him in.'

Sam got out his cell phone and called the Midnight Confessor's offices. Once he got the editor's desk, he asked for R. R. When he was told that R. R. was out on an assignment, Sam told him that he might have a lead on the missing newlyweds.

'I'll get a message out to him, pronto,' the editor responded. 'He knows that you and Jamie always have juicy stories. He'll be happy to return your call.'

Sam thanked the editor, and then began to plan his strategy for finding the missing trio.

He decided to use Rosita's Cantina as the center point of his search pattern. There were several places that fitted into his ideas of where people and vehicles could easily be hidden. If the trio were alive, then they would have to be fed at some point. There were several fast food restaurants and take-out places close to the old roadhouse. If he was right, there would be a pattern of purchases that would lead to the people that were holding the Jacksons and Mr. Erickson. This could be the mistake that would lead to closing the case.

★ ★ ★

About an hour after his call to the Midnight Confessor, Sam's phone vibrated.

'Sgt. Holmes,' he quickly answered. Even though the calling number was blocked, he was sure that it was R. R. calling.

'Detective,' the voice on the other end replied, 'R. R. returning your call. What have you got?'

'I need someone to help with a search grid,' Sam told his informer. 'I've got a fairly good idea of the area where our missing people may be hidden. I need someone who knows the territory and the people. Are you available?'

R. R. hesitated for about three seconds and said, 'What time and where do you want to meet?'

'Why don't I pick you up at your office,' Sam told him. 'Then we'll drive down to Rosita's Cantina.'

'Have they repaired the place since our last visit?' R. R. inquired, remembering the fire that had badly damaged the place.

'Yeah,' Sam told him, 'not that there's

been any improvements to speak of. There's a new bartender. She'll be right up your alley.'

'How so?'

'Ugly as a mud fence and friendly as a wildcat.'

'You really know how to hurt a guy!' R. R. groaned. 'Meet you in about an hour.'

Sam hung up and then went to the lieutenant's office. Lt. Baker waved him in as he saw Sam approach the office door.

'What have you got, Sam?' he asked.

'I'm going out to Rosita's on the eastern city limits to check on a hunch,' Sam answered. 'Jamie and I think that the area could be a hiding place for people, alive or dead. Jamie's got autopsy duty for the next couple of nights. Since R. R. knows the territory, I've invited him for a ride-along. Some of his contacts may be of help in the search, too.'

'You know that the department frowns on civilians being involved actively in an investigation, Sam,' was Baker's only comment.

'I know, but I think that I need him on this. I just want to have him talk to people so that I can maybe get lead.'

'My gut feeling says you're right, so I'll authorize it. If things start looking dicey, you get him out of harm's way. Understood?'

'Understood.'

* * *

About an hour later, Sam had parked in front of the repaired, but not remodeled, former roadhouse. They got out of their cars and walked in. The place still smelled of smoke, and the walls had been reinforced to meet minimum safety code standards, but it still looked ready to fall down. Behind the bar stood a woman weighing over two hundred pounds, bearing numerous tattoos, and looking meaner than most of the clientele.

'What did I tell you?' Sam said as they entered. 'She's right up your alley.'

'Not funny, Sergeant,' R. R. replied. 'Not *at all* funny.'

The shelves had been rebuilt with fire-resistant materials, and a fire-suppression system had been installed. Everything else still looked like it had been there since the prohibition era.

'Welcome to Rosita's Cantina,' the bartender greeted them. 'What's your poison tonight, gents?'

R. R. laid a twenty on the bar. 'Just a little information,' he said, keeping his fingers on the legal tender. 'We think some friends of ours may be stayin' around here. They may have a stretched lux for travelin'.'

'Ain't seen no stretched lux, but some guys been hangin' 'round that ain't been here before. They drop by about every night. Mean-lookin', even for in here. I had to bounce 'em outta here once or twice.'

'When did they start showing up?' Sam inquired, holding out his own twenty to go with R. R.'s.

'Less'n a week ago,' the answer came from the bartender. 'They always go just south of here when they leave. And another thing — I noticed several bags of fast food with 'em lots of times, like they's stayin' some place ain't got no cook stove.'

Sam let go of his twenty and R. R. did the same with his. The bartender made the bills disappear like in a magician's act.

'Thanks,' Sam said as he turned to go out the door.

'Better go out the back way,' R. R. whispered. 'Better sight lines.'

'Message received and understood.'

Two big and muscular men were waiting by the outdoor toilet as Sam and R. R. walked outside. The men looked them over, and then nodded to them. Sam recognized one of the customers from the fire. He was one of those that Sam's quick use of a fire extinguisher and the fire hose had saved that night from a fiery death.

'Evening, fellas,' he responded and kept on walking back to the parking lot where his car was parked.

'Those boyos you're lookin' for been stayin' out toward the old mine road,' the man said. 'There's a shack ain't been used in years there, but I seen some people go inside. Three of 'em. Two go inside and the other sits in the car, waitin' 'til they comes out. Then they drives off.'

'How often do they do this?' Sam asked nonchalantly.

R. R. reached into his pocket and pulled out another twenty.

The man who had been speaking held up his hand and shook his head. 'This is returnin' the favor,' he spoke calmly. 'No need to pay. These guys make a bad name for the place. The guys you want come just about dawn and again just before dark. They always have at least three big bags o' food with 'em. They don't stay long enough to eat. They got a lock on the door and they lock up when they leave.'

'Thanks,' Sam and R. R. said together. 'You may have saved some lives.'

'Like I said. Returnin' the favor.' The two men turned and walked back inside Rosita's.

Sam and R. R. reached a shack with blackout curtains just a short hike later. 'The old mine road is over there to the left,' R. R. pointed out. 'Looks like they don't want anybody seein' inside.'

'Those tracks in the gravel look new,' Sam observed. 'Someone's been here recently and often.'

'How can you tell?' R. R. quizzed. 'They just look like any old ruts to me.'

'We had a light, soaking rain a few nights ago. The newer tracks are slightly deeper and have the edges of gravel pushed up higher and still have some water in them. The really old ruts look slightly filled in and have more even edges. It'll be getting dark soon. I noticed a small stand of trees next to the road. Do you think we can hide from anyone coming to the shack?'

'Perhaps,' R. R. said after a short, intense observation of the surroundings.

The trees were about a hundred yards from the shack and fifty yards from the place where a car would need to turn on its approach to the shack. It appeared to be a perfect observation post in the gathering twilight.

Sam and R. R. had just reached a place of concealment when they heard the sound of a car headed toward them. The car had all of its lights off except the daytime running lights as it neared their hiding place.

The large Chevrolet sedan drove past them and turned toward the shack. Two caucasian men with very close haircuts and tattoos that said '187' on their forearms put on trench coats and ski masks and took several bags of food and several bottles of water inside the shack while an oriental-looking man waited in the car with the engine running while the shackled and blindfolded occupants were led out to the toilet. Three or four minutes after the people were returned to the shack, the two caucasians relocked the door. Without ever having said a word that Sam or R. R. could hear, the three men drove back the way they had come.

'Let's give them some time before we check out the shack,' Sam told R. R. 'It would be embarrassing if they came back before we could finish our reconnaissance.'

'Not only that,' R. R. said, sounding nervous, 'it could be downright dangerous.'

They waited twenty minutes before going to the door. 'This is a very simple lock,' Sam whispered, 'but it serves the purpose. It'll only take a few seconds to bypass it.'

Sam went to work on the lock while R. R. watched for the return of the Chevrolet. Less than a minute later, Sam had unlocked the door.

'Mr. and Mrs. Jackson?' Sam called out quietly as he eased open the door and turned on his flashlight. 'I'm Detective Sergeant Holmes of the LPD. Are you injured? Do you need medical assistance?'

'Mr. Erickson was battered and bruised when we were abducted, but once our leg shackles are removed, we should all be able to travel, Detective.' a female voice said from a darkened corner.

Sam focused the beam of his light in the direction of the voice. When he saw the three people, he aimed his light at their feet. 'Those look like standard police-issue leg cuffs,' he observed. 'I've got a key in my pocket. You should be free in just a few seconds.'

Sam took out his key for police hand

and ankle cuffs. Unfortunately, the key would not go into the locks. Smothering a four-letter word, he said to R. R., 'These cuffs must not be police standard. I'll have to either pick the locks or take a hacksaw to the chains. We may not have time for that.'

Taking his car keys from his pocket, he gave them to R. R. 'As quickly as you can,' he told his temporary partner, 'bring my car to the door. I'll help the Jacksons and Mr. Erickson get ready to leave. When we get back to headquarters, we can remove the leg cuffs without worrying about any interruptions.'

While R. R. went back to where they had left the car, Sam helped the three people gather what few belongings they had with them in the shack by the door for a quick transfer. As they waited, Sam took another look at their restraints with his flashlight.

'Your abductors have soldered the locks,' he reported, frustrated. 'No keys or lock picks will open them now. They'll have to be sawn or lasered off at the station. Fred and Judy will be notified as soon as we have you in a safe place. Mr. Erickson, do you have any idea where they may have taken your company's car?'

'Not really,' Erickson replied, a frown of concentration on his face. 'We was about half a mile from the William and Mary Grand Hotel when we stopped at a light. The car behind us ran into our back bumper. Two men jumped outta the back and the driver ran up to my window. The two from the back pointed guns at the Jacksons and made them stay in a back seat. The third had a short-barreled large-bore rifle pointed at me and made me roll down the glass. He could've had a shotgun, but I ain't shore.'

'What happened next?'

'When Mr. Erickson didn't roll the glass down fast enough, the man took the butt of his gun and slammed it through the window,' Sally Jackson took up the story. 'Then two of the men grabbed Mr. Erickson from the car, threw him on the ground and kicked him several times.'

'After that was when they pulled out three sets of shackles and put them around our ankles,' Mitch continued.

'They made us get into the back seat of their car and placed hoods over our heads. It seemed like it was a long time of driving before they stopped and led us into this shack.'

'Things weren't too bad,' Erickson added. 'They would bring food from several different fast-food places in large bags along with several bottles of water. There was plenty for the three of us.'

They heard a car's tires crunch outside on the gravel driveway. Sam carefully looked out from behind the door. He saw the car's headlights blink twice and then turn off. Sam recognized R. R. behind the wheel and quickly helped the trio reach the car and to get inside.

'Get us to the station without drawing attention to us,' he said to R. R. 'I'll call ahead and have someone with tools meet us and remove these chains.'

The ride to the police station was as silent as it was uneventful. There was no vehicle that seemed to be following them. R. R. pulled up to the police parking lot, where they were challenged at the gate. Sam showed the guard his badge and ID and explained their purpose for being at the station. He had also asked for any type of wheeled apparatus to help transport their three passengers as they approached the station.

As they were parking, three civilian assistants came toward them pushing wheelchairs. The Jacksons and Mr. Erickson were transferred to the chairs and taken inside to a conference room where Lt. Baker and a locksmith were waiting.

Fifteen minutes later, Fred and Judy were notified by phone that their parents were safe and could be picked up as soon as they had given their statements and the hospital had made certain that they were unharmed. Erickson's boss, Mr. Jacobs, was also informed of his employee's return and was told that he would be at the hospital while his injuries were being checked out. Neither of the Jacksons had been seriously harmed during their ordeal. They only needed a shower, clean clothes, and some time to recuperate from their imprisonment.

'Your parents are fine,' Lt. Baker told

the younger Jacksons when they arrived. 'After they've had time to rest, we'll need to ask them questions about their abductors and their abduction. Mr. Erickson will be under observation at the hospital for a day or two, and he'll also need to give us any information he has.'

'When can we take them home?' Fred inquired of the lieutenant.

'They should be finishing their statements soon.' Lt. Baker was glad that things had turned out so well for the Jacksons and Mr. Erickson.

9

By midnight, all of the abductees had been released from their shackles and the elder Jacksons had finished their interviews. Mr. Erickson had been seen by the doctor on call at the hospital and had been admitted for observation. He had elected to give his interview after being examined and placed in his room.

'I need time to gather my wits,' he explained.

Sam met Jamie in the corridor outside the corridor the autopsy room lobby and told her the events of the evening. 'The driver was the only one who was injured?' Jamie asked. 'The Jacksons were just intimidated and then shackled and put in the old shack?'

'Yes,' Sam answered. 'They both stated that only one time were they touched other than to be shackled and then assisted into and out of the car and into the shack. Neither of them had any explanation for Mr. Erickson's treatment other than perhaps they felt he was being too slow in following their instructions. I think they also wanted to make sure the Jacksons were cowed into instant obedience.'

'And the company limo?' Jamie wanted to know. 'What was done with the car?'

'None of the victims actually saw it being driven away.' Sam looked at his interview notes. 'But all three of them reported hearing the limo sounding like it was being driven back the way they had come before the Chevy started to move. We've placed a BOLO on the vehicle within a five-mile radius of the William and Mary. We're also checking all of the known chop and body shops in the same area. It's unlikely that the car would have been taken very far. A limo with FFTS-1 vanity plates from the Fair Fare Transport Services would be too high-profile.'

* * *

Before he headed home, Sam checked his computer for messages. He found an update from Lt. Baker about the last case that Tom Jenkins had worked on before his death.

'American Investigations stated that the case was dropped because Tom's notes went missing,' the message read. 'The client decided not to proceed with the case. Suggest you see what his widow remembers, if anything.' Sam printed out the computer message and then left the squad room.

Early the next day, Sam called the Jacksons and asked them to meet him at the Mom and Pop's coffee shop in an hour. 'I need to ask some questions about Tom's last case,' he told them. 'It may be related to the abduction.'

All four of the Jacksons arrived together just a few minutes after Sam and Jamie. They pushed a couple of tables together and sat down. 'Sally,' Sam began, 'according to the office manager in charge of cases at American Investigations, Tom's last case was dropped by the client after his death and his notes on the investigation disappeared. Did Tom ever hypothesize about his cases with you?'

'He'd sometimes mention that a case had him puzzled,' Sally said after a moment, 'and then later say that something had fallen into place and he'd soon be finished and turning in his final report. We never talked details about his work. Just how things were working out in general.'

'Was he ever fretful, or did he seem anxious, about the direction a case was taking?' Sam questioned. 'Did he ever carry a weapon? His company said that he had a permit to carry a concealed weapon.'

'He almost never wore his gun unless he was working as armed security at a site for highly sensitive materials,' Sally replied. 'He worked several times for the transportation division: moving valuable artwork, making payroll deliveries, transporting prisoners, deporting illegals. That sort of thing.'

'What about the case he was working on at the time of his accident?'

'It was just an information gathering case.' Sally frowned. 'Why are you asking about Tom's accident?'

'None of the investigators were positive it wasn't a planned affair,' Jamie told Sally. 'We're just trying to put together anything that may have had to do with you and Mitch being abducted. It's highly unlikely that the kidnappers would snatch someone and then not notify the family of their demands for several days. Especially when the victims were being kept in reasonably good health.'

'Are you trying to say that one of us planned our own kidnapping?' Mitch was incensed. 'And on our wedding night, of all nights?'

'We're not saying anything yet,' Sam replied, trying to deflect Mitch's anger. 'Our investigation is still at the information-gathering stage right now. Anything that even remotely relates to why either of you were targeted could help us find the perpetrators.'

While Sam's answer calmed Mitch's anger, it did little to settle Mitch's mind or relieve his sense of being a suspect.

Fred and Judy looked on with bewilderment in their faces. Judy looked as though she would rather be anywhere but where she was. She looked at her mother and then at her husband, Fred. 'The night before Pop was killed,' she hesitantly interrupted, 'he came to talk to me in my room. He was acting a little strangely. First, he hugged me as though he never expected to be with me again. Then he made me promise that I would take care of you, Mom, if something should happen to him. After the accident, it felt like he had had a premonition something bad would happen.'

With tears in her eyes, Sally looked at her daughter. 'You never said anything about this before,' she sobbed. 'Why wait until now?'

'I thought that you had enough grief,' Judy replied. 'And I figured that you might feel guilty that he didn't feel that he could confide in you. That maybe you had let him down somehow.'

Mother and daughter reached out to console each other while the others looked on. After they finally let get go, Jamie asked the two women the question that had come to her mind. 'Tom was obviously concerned that something he had discovered could put him in danger,' she said thoughtfully. 'Yet he never hinted at his worries until the night before his death?'

'Knowing the line of work he was in,' Fred Jackson chimed in, 'would that have been unusual? I mean, wouldn't he have tried to keep his wife and daughter from undue worry?'

'Yes, that would be the most likely scenario,' Sam replied. 'However, maybe he might have believed that this time was unlike any other he had faced and began thinking about how Sally and Judy would be supported in a future without him. Did he make any changes to his will, or in how the finances were arranged?'

'He did change a CD account from his name to a trust fund in Judy's name that was to be given to her on her wedding day or her twenty-fifth birthday, which ever came first, as a gift,' Sally said after thinking for a minute. 'She was graduating from high school and was turning eighteen just two weeks later. He told me that he felt that it wouldn't be very long before she left the nest and that he wanted her to have a good start.'

'How large was this gift?'

'It was about $10,000,' Judy replied. 'Fred and I placed it in our special account toward the down payment for our future home purchase. It hasn't had time to grow very much yet. With home prices back on the rise, we were waiting until we had doubled or tripled our savings.'

'And what about Mitch's proposal to allow you to take over the mortgage payments on his house instead of putting one, or both, houses on the market?'

'That was something that Sally and I were talking to the kids about before the wedding,' Mitch answered. 'Fred and Judy were going to let us know their thoughts when we returned from our honeymoon. We had already decided to live in Sally's house so that her customers wouldn't have to travel anywhere else that might have cost her business. She would also save on the cost of renting a space for her shop.'

'Wouldn't your retirement income and the equities from both of your houses have made up for any extra cost or the loss of some of her clientele?' asked Jamie.

'And then some,' Sally told her. 'But I had put in ten years building my client base and neither of us felt that a move at this time was worth the loss of any of my long-term customers.'

'Can anyone think of any reason that would benefit someone if Sally or Mitch disappeared at this time?' Sam tried to get them to think about the people in their circle of friends, acquaintances, or customers who would see any of them as an obstacle or as an enemy. All four of the Jacksons looked at one another, and then shook their heads.

'So where does that leave us, Detective?' Fred asked.

One of two places,' Sam replied. 'Either someone feels threatened by the reopening of the investigation into Tom's 'accident', or someone has a grudge against the limo company or someone in its employ.'

'What about Mitch's old place of work?' Sally queried. 'Could someone there be jealous of his retirement income?'

'We are making discrete inquiries into that possibility,' Jamie answered. 'We're also looking into the possibility he may have left behind a disgruntled customer or two when he left.'

10

After all of the questions had been asked and considered, the Jacksons had all left to return to their homes and Sam and Jamie stayed behind to discuss what they had learned.

'Sally asked a good question about Mitch's workplace,' Jamie said as they reviewed possibilities. 'What if someone is jealous or holding a grudge?'

'But why wait three years to do something about it?' Sam pondered. 'I know the old saying about revenge being a dish best served cold. Maybe it's the company and not just one employee. I still think one of Tom's last cases was used to set him up.'

'And why go after Sally?' Jamie wondered. 'Is there some connection between one of the cases that Tom was investigating and Mitch, or his company, that we aren't looking at?'

'You could be onto something, Jamie.'

Sam was thoughtful as he considered what Jamie had just said. 'Let's get back to the squad room and check out which company was Tom's client, and which company was being investigated.'

As they drove back toward City Hall and Police Headquarters, Sam mused, *At least no one has tried to shoot or stab one of us yet on this case. Things happened just a little too quickly with the super-Taser case.*

As he turned south from King George Avenue onto Central Boulevard, a bronze Ford F250 stake-bed pick-up came out of the gas station, tires smoking as its passed in front of him. Sam jammed on his brakes and swerved to his right and into the gas station, barely avoiding a collision.

'Call 911!' the station attendant yelled as he came out of his booth. 'I've just been robbed!'

'We're police officers!' Jamie told him. 'We'll call it in. Were they the people in the stake-bed?'

'Yes,' the attendant replied. 'They had guns.'

Sam called dispatch and reported the

robbery. He quickly gave description of the vehicle and warned responding officers about the suspects being armed and that they should be considered dangerous.

After reporting the last known direction of the F250, he and Jamie took a preliminary report from the now pale and shaky attendant. Jamie calmed the attendant until he could give a coherent report.

'There were three of 'em,' the attendant, who was in his late teens or early twenties, was finally able to tell her. 'The two passengers who got out and came to the booth were both around six feet tall. One was slightly heavier than the other. Both were wearing Grunge-style jeans, calf-high hunting boots, and long-sleeved heavy T-shirts with the logo '187' printed on the backs. Their baseball caps hid most of their faces, but I could tell that they were caucasian. The third fella got out and pumped $20 worth of gas while the other two were at the booth. He looked oriental and was dressed like the other guys, but he might have been a bit shorter.'

'You said that they had guns,' Sam said as he joined Jamie in the interview with the attendant. 'Did they speak to you? Did they have an accent?'

'No,' the young man stated. 'They stuck the guns in my face and handed a printed note through the cash slot. It said that they wanted all of the money in the cash register and that their guns had armor-piercing loads.'

'And you believed them.' Jamie's remark was more of a statement than a question.

'*Of course* I believed 'em.' The attendant wiped his mouth on his sleeve. 'The boss had told all of us to comply with robbers. They always said the money was insured and could be replaced, but people's lives couldn't.'

'What else did the boss tell you?' Sam wanted to know.

'Stay calm, remember as much as possible, and don't provoke an incident.'

'Any security cameras on the premises?'

'One at both ends of each island, and one aimed just over my shoulder.'

'We're going to need the recordings,' Jamie told him. 'Is there any chance we can take them with us?'

'I'm sure the boss will want to cooperate when I tell him what happened. Especially since I know the patrol officers who just pulled in.'

Two officers stepped out of their cruiser and walked over to the booth. The lead officer recognized Sam and relaxed his countenance. He spoke to his partner and told her that the two people standing with the attendant were detectives from headquarters.

'Hey, Joe,' he greeted the attendant, 'what d'ya know?'

'That I don't like guns pointed in my face!' was the nervous reply. 'Especially when the perps wieldin' them are usin' armor-piercing bullets! Two-inch-thick plexiglass ain't gonna stop that kind of bullet!'

'You sure, Joe?' asked the younger officer, her eyebrow raised in surprise.

'They shoved a note under the glass

that said so, Shirley,' he answered. 'I wasn't gonna disbelieve what it said. You know what I mean?'

'Yeah,' her partner agreed. 'We know *exactly* what you mean. Better get on the radio and alert the others with the update.'

'Right away, Jack,' Shirley replied as she returned to their unit.

'How about that permission on the video records?' Sam asked. 'We need to look at them ASAP.'

'I'll call the boss right now,' Joe said. 'I'm sure he'll want to cooperate. After all, anything that gets recovered, the insurance company doesn't have to cover and that'll help keep his premiums down.' Joe made his call and five minutes later he was turning over the recordings of the robbery.

Sam took out his cell phone and, using his photo application, took pictures of the tire marks left by the fleeing vehicle. He knew that forensics would also take pictures and make measurements. He also took pictures of the skid marks he had made in avoiding the suspect vehicle.

Joe sat down with the uniformed officers and, with the help of their questioning, gave as much detail as he remembered for their report. Sam and Jamie each wrote out everything that had happened from the time the truck had nearly hit them until Jack and Shirley had arrived.

★　★　★

The videos from the security cameras had gotten clear pictures of the suspects, their vehicle, and the license plate. As expected, the stake-bed was soon found abandoned just outside the city limits in an old unused vineyard.

The interior of the truck had been set afire, and the heat had made forensic examination of the exterior impossible until the metal had cooled once the fire was put out.

'The heat from the fire may have evaporated or distorted any finger or palm prints left on the outside,' the forensic examiner stated while they waited. 'And the interior is pretty well trashed. Everybody who watches CSI thinks that makes them some kinda crime guru, but everyone slips up somewhere.'

'Get us what you can,' the lead investigator from the Robbery Division sighed in frustration. 'What do we know about any gangs using the '187' designation?'

'Aside from it being the police call sign for a homicide, some gangs use the graffiti to designate the kills of people from other territories that were on the wrong turf,' Sam offered, 'but I have never heard of a gang using it for a name.'

'Maybe it's like that old Diana Rigg movie, *Murder Incorporated*,' Jamie offered. 'You know, a corporation of professional hit men.'

'That sounds too much like a mystery thriller to be real life,' the robbery detective commented derisively.

'Eliminate the impossible — ' Sam started to say.

'And whatever is left, however improbable,' Jamie continued, 'must be the truth.'

'Sometimes,' Sam smiled, 'there are things to be learned from mystery tales, even from a hundred and fifty years ago.'

11

Sam and Jamie had R. R. meet them in the city library's conference room the next day as early as possible. R. R and the two detectives arrived about five minutes after the doors to the library were opened. With a look of puzzlement, R. R. asked what was going on.

'We got everyone back, basically unhurt, didn't we?' he questioned. 'That's what we wanted, wasn't it?'

'Yes it was,' Sam told him. 'However, that wasn't all. We need to learn why the victims were chosen and how the timing of the kidnapping fits in. We want to put away as many people involved in this as we can.'

'Okay.' The tabloid reporter shrugged. 'What d'you need me from me?'

'Just be your usual sleazy self,' Jamie replied, 'and find out anything related to Jenkins or any of the Jacksons that you can.'

'Remember those tattoos on the two guys we saw delivering the food to that shack?' Sam asked. 'The ones on their forearms that said '187'?'

'What about 'em?'

'Three guys who held up a gas station yesterday were wearing T-shirts with the same logo on the backs. I think there may be a connection. Anything you can find out could be important to the larger picture.'

'Okay,' R. R. replied after thinking a moment. 'I'll have 'Johnny' poke around and see what he can stir up.'

The three of them discussed theories, possibilities, and tactics for another twenty minutes and then each headed out to put their area of expertise to work. Jamie headed back to the police building to do a search on the police computers for anything in the data banks on the term '187' as it related to any known activities of criminal groups. Sam had decided to return to the Medical Supply Superstore to see if he could ferret out anything new relating to Mitch Jackson and his company relationships at the time of his retirement, especially how the retirement package and his stated reasons for leaving affected co-workers and his personal customer accounts.

R. R. became 'Johnny Oh' and checked the streets for any information related to the gang logo '187'.

★ ★ ★

Johnny took the bus southeast of the Kings and Queens Avenues toward Joe's Bar and Grill. He had contacts there that knew him, but not his alter ego, R. R. the reporter. He also had contacts that knew R. R the reporter but not Johnny Oh the information broker. He decided the risk was worth the possible losses of to the reputation of either or both personas.

He walked in and took a careful look around, checking to see if any of Johnny's contacts were nearby. Then he checked again for R. R.'s known associates. Finding neither, Johnny sat down at the bar and ordered a beer.

'You seen Slash or Bash 'round lately?' he asked the bartender.

'Not for a coupla days,' the man behind the bar said. 'Everybody's been walkin' on eggshells since Maxie took over the South territory. They're just waitin' to see which way to jump.'

'Yeah,' Johnny replied, 'I been outta circulation for a while an' I didn't get back 'til last week. I ran into Slash an' he told me 'bout the changes. Then Maxie's boys took me to see him. We made the same deal I had with Stonewall.'

'So, what're you lookin' for?'

'I been hearin' 'bout these gangers that are mebbe callin' themselves the '187'. You ever hear of 'em?'

The bartender rubbed his chin and then said, 'Can't say that I have. I been seein' some tattoos, though. Why you askin'?'

'Could be they wanna make a move on Maxie,' R. R. told him in a conspiratorial tone of voice. 'Mebbe Maxie'll throw somethin' my way if I can tell him 'bout them.'

'Yeah,' the other man grinned. 'He might be grateful at that.'

101

'You remember what these dudes look like?'

'Well, I only seen three or four of 'em.' The bartender frowned. 'Some was white guys with real short haircuts, but I don't think they was skinheads. They had some Asiatics, too. Short haircuts, too, but no tattoos other than the '187'. He paused, then added: 'Oh yeah. One did have a dragon with nine heads tattooed on the back of his left hand.'

'Thanks, Mac.' Johnny placed a twenty on the bar for his beer walked toward the door. Then he turned back and said with his finger against his lips, 'Just our little secret.'

* * *

Sam pulled into the empty space across the street from the Medical Supply Superstore and sat for a few moments considering his options.

What was Mitch Jackson really like, I wonder? Sam asked himself. *Mr. Zeiter wasn't all that informative during our last interview. I wonder if he would allow*

*interviews with Mitch's coworkers. I'll
need to talk with some of the people from
his former accounts, as well.*

Having decided on a course of inquiry,
Sam got out of his vehicle and entered
the store. He was again greeted by the
man he had first met during his last visit.

'Good afternoon, Detective,' he greeted
Sam cordially, but without sincerity. 'Are
you looking for Mr. Zeiter?'

'In a moment,' Sam answered. 'Did you
know Mitch Jackson while his wife was
ill?'

'I was transferred to this store about six
months before Mrs. Jackson passed away,'
the man said. 'The previous store
manager had just received a promotion
and I was brought in to close the gap.'

'So you were his immediate supervisor
during his last six or seven months of
active employment?' Sam questioned.
'What kind of employee was he? Was he a
productive salesman or was he only
mediocre?'

The store manager frowned and his
posture showed his uneasiness. 'Mitch
had an enviable record before I arrived,'

he informed Sam. 'Before his wife's battle with cancer, he would most likely have become the new store manager. Understandably, after the doctors had diagnosed her as terminal, his work began to deteriorate. The needs of his wife began to take more and more of his time and energy. If his record hadn't been what it was, he wouldn't have received the leniency he did.'

'What about his working relationships?' Sam was curious. 'Were there any feelings that Mr. Jackson was receiving preferential or special treatment?'

'There may have been some,' Sam was told. 'Some people naturally felt some anger and that they were being pressured to take up the slack in Mitch's perceived drop in performance. That would only have been natural. I myself felt that, rather than allow his record to suffer, he should have been forced to take the hardship leave he'd been offered so that he could attend to his family affairs.'

'Was there anyone in particular who was exceptionally vocal about his feelings, or showed hostility toward Mr. Jackson's 'preferential treatment'?'

'There was one of our salesmen who left our employ voluntarily,' the manager offered. 'He stated that the work environment was no longer conducive to productivity. He was also on the shortlist for the next round of layoffs.'

'Was he a bad employee?'

'Not really. He was the least senior of our sales staff.' The manager was beginning to act as if he thought he was saying more than he should. 'Anything else, Detective?'

'No,' Sam responded, correctly reading the other's body language that said to continue the interview would be unproductive. 'If Mr. Zeiter is available now, I'd like to see him.'

* * *

Jamie sat at her desk, reviewing the hits her search engines had produced on the term '187'. Other than the information she already knew, she received nothing. Frustrated, she typed in a new search using the parameters 'Murder Inc.,'

'Death Inc.,' and '187 Inc.' She got three hits. One was the movie she had remembered when first told about the tattoos and T-shirt logos. The second referred to an obscure but elite squad of snipers from the Vietnam era. The third sounded like what she was looking for.

'187 Inc.' was the name of a highly militant group of supposed separatists who offered their skills as assassins to the highest bidder from other anti-establishment fringe groups. The organization also had its own lists of targets according to the FBI, the Secret Service, the Department of Homeland Security, and other watchers of homegrown terrorists.

How did Mitch and Sally come to be noticed by this gang? Jamie asked herself. She decided that she needed more information on the backgrounds of Jenkins and all of the Jacksons. *Too many of the puzzle pieces are fitting together from seemingly unrelated puzzles.* She got up from her desk and walked to Lt. Baker's office.

'I need a few minutes, Lieutenant,' she said after being told to enter the office.

'What have you got, Jamie?' Baker asked, pointing to an empty chair.

'The results of a law enforcement search engine.' Jamie slid a printout of the '187 Inc.' search and put it on his desk. 'I don't think we have a simple kidnapping anymore.'

As the lieutenant looked over the hard copy, Jamie also handed him a file on the death of Tom Jenkins. 'Tom Jenkins's death is beginning to look less and less like a drunk-driving accident.' Jamie began to tell Baker about Judy's revelations of her father's behavior shortly before his death and his leaving the trust account toward her future.

'From what Judy and her mother said,' Judy continued, 'he may have intuited that something was different about this particular case, and he wanted his wife and daughter to be taken care of. Tom had always paid extra on the principle of the house. That's why the loan was so close to being paid off. The life insurance he had was enough to make the final payments all at once. The settlement from his company's insurance and his own made certain that she wouldn't have to sell her home or business to live. Judy's trust fund was enough to give her a good start when she married.'

'So,' Baker inquired, 'do you believe that this group was hired to kill Jenkins?'

'I'm not sure,' Jamie answered. 'I only have a weak tie-in between Tom's death and Sally's kidnapping. I'm going to need to ask all of the Jacksons new and searching questions. I hope Tom's agency will be more forthcoming after we tell them what we have now.'

'Maybe this will help them decide to share,' Baker said as he dismissed Jamie.

As she left, she saw Lt. Baker dial an inside line.

'Captain?' Baker said as the other end of the line was picked up. 'This is Lt. Baker over in Homicide. Our A-team may have found a connection to that recent kidnapping and a cold case from three years ago.' Baker told Captain Reynolds everything that Jamie's computer search had discovered for any group using the term '187' and her conclusions. 'Sally Jackson's late husband may have been investigating more than just industrial espionage,' he concluded. 'None of the official investigations were totally convinced that his death was just vehicular manslaughter caused by a drunk driver. Holmes and Watson's confidential informant found a witness to the accident three years ago who believes that the driver veered into the path of Jenkins's car purposefully and are seeking to verify his information. Holmes is doing more Q and A of Mitch's former associates from his place of business. He and Dr. Watson are also asking for more details about the last case that Jenkins was working on.'

'I'll see what our friends at American Investigations will be willing to trade for this new information,' Captain Reynolds said. 'Maybe we can get a little quid pro quo. I'll check with the Department of Justice, too. They may want a piece of the action and possibly be willing to share. If not, Dr. Watson seems very good at getting what she wants from the internet. We'll give her free rein for her info searches and go with what she gets.'

Lt. Baker hung up his phone and began his weekly written reports of all of his detectives' investigations.

12

Sam, Jamie, and R. R. had agreed to meet at Johanna's that evening between the dinner rush and the late-night fun-seeker crowds' arrival. Jamie had arrived first. Johanna seated her in her and Sam's usual booth. 'Are you here for business or pleasure tonight, Jamie?' she inquired as she signaled a waiter to come to the table. 'Will Sam be joining you tonight?'

'We'll also be joined by a third person for an information sharing session, Jamie told her, 'so yes, it'll be mostly business tonight.'

'Just be sure you keep control of your pet.' Johanna had spied R. R. coming through the door. 'He's barely housebroken.'

'Do you think that a swat to the nose with a rolled-up newspaper will help teach him his manners?' Jamie quizzed.

'Naw,' Johanna laughed. 'He's as dumb as mud.'

R. R. slid into the booth across from Jamie. 'I'm glad someone finds somethin' to laugh at about,' he said as he settled down into his seat. 'I've just about walked m' feet to death.'

'Too bad you didn't talk your lips to death.' Sam slid in beside R. R. 'That would give our ears a well-deserved rest.' Everyone had a laugh at Sam's comment.

'It cost me a hundred bucks,' R. R. exclaimed, 'but I think got some leads on the '187' mob.'

Sam and Jamie got serious looks on their faces as they gauged R. R.'s validity. 'Sorry,' Jamie apologized, 'but you're so much fun to tease.'

'Yes,' Sam added. 'Go ahead and go first with what you've learned.'

'Well,' R. R., still miffed at the teasing, began his report, 'these guys are either ex-military or military wannabes. They're mostly of WASP or Asian descent. I think even Maxie and his people step off of the sidewalk when they see them comin'. That, or turn around and walk the other way.'

'That fits in with the little I've found

out from the internet,' Jamie told the guys. 'According to Lawenforcement.gov, Death Inc. was the unofficial designation given to the elite sniper squadrons of Vietnam and both Gulf wars. Then, two or three years ago, there were rumors of a murder-for-hire group that referred to itself as '187 Inc.'. They're an exclusive group that seems to be as tight-knit as they are deadly. Lt. Baker is doing some follow-up for us.'

'Now,' Sam said as he leaned back in the booth, 'we need to make the connection between Tom Jenkins's death, the Jackson's kidnappings, and 187 Inc. Mitch Jackson incurred a lot of debt during his first wife's battle with cancer and turned several of his friends and supporters into either very upset or neutral associates.'

'Were you able to find out more on Tom Jenkins's accident, Jamie? R. R.?'

'Only that American Investigations is still calling it an unresolved vehicular death and that that it's been moved from a drunk driver involved fatality to an open/unresolved investigation at their headquarters. It seems that no one is satisfied with the initial investigation. Do you think someone was trying to get this swept under the rug?'

'Could be,' R. R. spoke up. 'I found someone else besides Jerry the Rummy who remembers the accident. Little Sawhorse claimed that he was doin' some carpentry work 'bout a block southeast o' where Tom's Ford was creamed. Said that there was this clunker with some dude sittin' in it.

'About ten minutes before the crash, he sees the guy talkin' on a cell phone. When he's done, the guy drowns a bunch o' pills with a bottle o' booze. Then he heads north on Jane toward the Laun-Dro-Matic on tenth. My guy watches the parkin' lot until he sees the clunker peel onto tenth headed east. When the blue Ford comes into view toward him, the driver my guy's bin watchin' swerves into the westbound lane, headed straight for the Ford. The two slam head-on and there's an explosion and fire. My man knows that there's no way everyone's not a crispy critter inside, so he runs before the law, fire crews and docs arrive. He said it was mighty peculiar how things happened with nobody else seein' anything and all.'

'According to the original report,' Sam said, 'A quick-thinking business owner with a fire extinguisher kept the fire from spreading to the buildings and saved enough of the two bodies for forensics to make any kind of identification and evidence report possible.'

'Now the million dollar questions,' Jamie reflected. 'Why was Tom Jenkins singled out? Or was he an unfortunate victim of mistaken identity? And who was the other driver?'

'The accident report claimed that he had no identification,' Sam answered. 'The car he was driving had no license plate, all other personal and vehicle identification was either destroyed or missing, and there was no record of his DNA or dental records being on file.'

'Okay.' Sam signaled the waiter to bring the bill. 'Everyone continue their current line of inquiry. It looks like we may be all headed in the right directions.'

'Our guests had help,' the caucasian man in the black T-shirt with tattooed and muscular forearms told the gray-haired man with a military bearing. 'The locks were picked. We also noted some tire tracks leading up to and away from the shack's front door. Since the cuffs all had solder in the locks, we figure that they were put into the car and driven to where they could be cut off without bein' interrupted.'

'Our client is not happy.' The older man glared at his three underlings. 'Your fellows have paid for their stupid, ill-advised and ill-timed robbery. A mere two hundred and fifty-five dollars and twenty dollars of gas was not worth having our operations revealed. The softening-up of the widow was taking too long with the police sniffing around as quickly as they did. She and her companions should have been moved. Another costly mistake.

'Three years ago, we believed that our client's interests had been satisfied and that this wouldn't be a problem for later. Now we, and they, are at risk of exposure that we can ill afford at this time. You three and your three friends have become liabilities instead of assets.'

From underneath the desk, the gray-haired leader pulled out a .45 automatic and quickly fired three silenced shots into the chests of the men seated in front of him. The fractal ammunition splintered inside their hearts, causing the almost instant deaths of his victims.

'I need a trash pick-up and clean-up crew in my office,' he said as he pressed the talk button on his desk intercom. 'Oh, and see how soon the carpet and chair upholstery can be replaced.'

Moments later, a crew wearing gloves and splatter suits came in and began the removal of the bodies. 'Should we place the trash in the incinerator?' the crew foreman asked.

'Yes,' he was told. 'And make sure everything is consumed completely. I want it all turned to ash. There's to be nothing left for identification.'

Except for three light pink stains in the

carpet and the upholstery of the three guest chairs, the office showed no signs of violence thirty minutes later. The carpet and chairs were to be replaced within forty-eight hours.

Two new teams of three each were called into an adjoining office, where the leader of 187 Inc. glared at them. 'The six members whose stupidity, negligence, and incompetence have endangered this corporation have been terminated from our employ with extreme prejudice,' he informed them. 'Now we must clean up after them. Besides the two original targets, we now must add at least six more: the limo driver, the reporter, the two cops, and the original targets' children. All of these people have now become dangerously involved in our business affairs and therefore need to be neutralized. The police officers are the most dangerous. They have the unfortunate, for us, combination of tenacity, luck, and learning from generations of practical experience. Their removal is top priority. Everyone else is to be neutralized as opportunity avails itself, but these two have the capacity to eliminate our efforts. *Do not fail!*'

Both teams heard the implied '*or else!*' as they left the office with the cold expressions of the Grim Reaper himself on their faces. The first team headed toward the square mile in center of the city where Sam and Jamie were known to spend most of their working and leisure hours. The second team headed for the north-central area north of Gemson Avenue where the two houses of the elder Jacksons were located.

Neither of the two teams was surprised to hear about the teams that they were replacing. The snatch job and the gas station hold-up had been impromptu or rush-jobs of opportunity instead of well-planned and thought-out efforts.

13

As Sam and Jamie walked toward the exit after leaving the cash register, Hamish, one of Johanna's greeters, said to them in an aside, 'Three men in a black Chevrolet SUV across the street. Been there for at least fifteen minutes. They keep looking this way, but not getting out or leaving.'

'Did you call it in?' Sam asked. 'I'm always suspicious of people watching a cop bar.'

'So am I,' Hamish replied, and then continued, 'I told Johanna several minutes ago and she called it in. The cruiser should be through here anytime. Twenty-five years workin' patrol and detective bureaus give me an itch between my shoulder blades when I see things like this.'

'Thanks, Hamish,' Jamie said. 'Here comes the patrol unit now.'

The patrol cruiser drove down the street, the officers watching the parked vehicles on both sides of the street. As they approached the black SUV, it started up and pulled slowly into traffic.

'Looks like we'll make it to our cars without incident now,' R. R. remarked as he walked out the door.

Sam looked up the street in the direction that the SUV had driven off. As he started to follow R. R., he saw the Chevy SUV head toward them on their side of the street. Grabbing R. R. by his collar and pulling him back inside and onto the floor, he heard the 'thump-thump' of the tires as they jumped the curb onto the sidewalk. As the SUV passed Johanna's door, two shotgun blasts blew out the beveled glass. Fifteen seconds later, red and blue flashing lights and the wail of a siren went by in hot pursuit.

'I should've stayed with the family clientele,' Johanna complained loudly. 'I thought having cops for customers would give me some protection from this sorta thing. My insurance is already through the roof! Much more of this and I won't be able to buy insurance at any price!'

One of the detectives at a nearby booth chimed in, 'We'll take up a collection to fix the door, Johanna. This is the best place in the city for us to relax or talk shop.'

'The best grilled steaks anywhere, too,' one of his companions added.

'Okay, ladies and gentlemen,' Johanna said as she glared at them, 'the last time I had to replace that door, it cost me three hundred dollars plus labor. You want me to stay in business as a cop and family grill and bar, then you all had better divvy up. Especially the three of you, Sam. You're all disaster magnets!'

Then she gave them all a mischievous grin as she pulled out a wide-mouthed gallon jug and labeled a large Post-it note and then stuck it on the jug. 'Besides the tip jar, there will now be now be a repair donation jar and a mandatory one percent surcharge on the bill for any bill over fifteen bucks for all police officers. If that don't cover my repair bills from violence, then I'll have to extend that to all customers. Maybe that'll make every-one more careful about the kinda trouble they bring into my place.'

No one was willing to argue with her as she placed the gallon jug with the sign stating the new policy one the counter. 'The policy begins *now!*' she said. 'Voluntary contributions cheerfully accepted.'

Sam, Jamie, and R. R. were the first to donate to the jar. 'We each put in twenty bucks,' Jamie told the crowd. 'Let's see how many of you are willing to match us to keep Johanna from throwing us out.'

'I hope you don't expect this kinda donation every night!' one of the regulars quipped.

'Just the one percent surcharge if your bill is over fifteen dollars, Jonesy,' Johanna answered.

★ ★ ★

'Johanna sure was steamed,' R. R. noted as they walked out to the parking lot. 'I think I'll stay out of her way for a few days. Like, maybe a year!'

'She'll get over it,' Sam offered his opinion. 'Just don't expect the damages jar or the surcharge to go away. That's the third time in twelve months that she's had to have repairs done to her place. It's either the surcharge for us or an increase in her prices across the board. She makes too much profit on the family business to price them out of her place.'

'What about the surcharge for the peace officers?' Jamie asked. 'Won't she lose money anyway if they stop coming in?'

'They're the ones most of the damages can be attributed to because of the enemies that those same officers have made,' Sam replied. 'The non-law-abiding people of this city and the just plain angry or ornery folks with a beef against the establishment seem to have gotten to be more volatile in recent times. That makes places like Johanna's more vulnerable.'

'Do you think the family clientele will make voluntary contributions?' R. R. queried the two.

'I think so,' Jamie told him. 'Even with the drive-by violence of recent years, most people feel safer with a room full of cops.'

The conversation inside Johanna's had

settled down to murmurings and whispers by the time the trio once more made their exit. 'Life sure is excitin' hangin' with the two of you,' R. R. stated as they approached their cars. 'I've been threatened with bodily harm, almost set on fire, run over by a car, and now I've been shot at! And I ain't known neither of you for a year yet!'

'Such is the life of fame.' Jamie made an exaggerated sigh and shrugged her shoulders. 'Our ancestors of the nineteenth century got the notoriety, and every generation since has had at least one member from each family that followed suit.'

'I often wonder what it would have been like,' Sam added, 'to have been related to a quieter set of people. Might be nice having regular ancestors. Nice and quiet.'

'And dull as dishwater,' Jamie laughed.

'That, too.'

14

'The limousine was found in the stone quarry at the southwest section of the city late yesterday afternoon,' Lt. Baker told Sam and Jamie soon after they arrived in the squad room the next morning. 'Forensics started checking it over at about midnight. We should hear the results at about four o'clock.'

'After what happened last night,' Sam said, running his hand through his hair, 'I think someone's getting nervous.'

'I heard about the disturbance at Johanna's.' Lt. Baker looked at his young detectives. 'Was that the two of you?'

'Our reports will be on your desk by noon,' Jamie replied. 'Unfortunately, Johanna is now having police officers pay a one percent surcharge on all checks over the amount of fifteen dollars. She also put up a jar for voluntary contributions for repairs to her place.'

Lt. Baker gave a sad shake of his head

as he woefully remarked, 'Everything keeps going up, except our budget! Our overtime budget's been cut again, and they won't budge on salary increases.' As he dismissed the detective team, he added, 'Keep up the good work with the investigations. The captain may have something for you from American Investigations later today.'

★ ★ ★

In the abandoned warehouse on the corner of Tenth and Taft Avenues, several tough-looking men and women were gathering secretly. All of them had a tattoo of the number '187' somewhere that could be easily hidden and yet quickly exposed upon need for identification. The tough exterior of each person was seemingly one of confidence in their ability to neutralize any physical threat, much the same way an expert in the martial arts would have. The exception for these individuals lay in the cold demeanor behind their eyes and the way their smiles never reflected any human warmth.

The man in front of the room could have passed for the chief executive of any global corporation. His graying hair, military bearing and self-assurance commanded respect from this elite group. He approached the head of the conference table, sat down, and called the meeting to order. 'Our efforts of late for our client,' he began without preliminaries, 'have met with some reversals. Efforts have begun to correct these backward steps. The effects of these endeavors should make themselves felt by our competitors very soon. Our other projects have not been affected by these minor setbacks so far and are keeping pace with our timetables. New projects are being considered at this very moment and should be most lucrative.

'Our support of our fellow entrepreneurs has been successful and we are attracting more business. With the exception of a few individuals who insist on interfering with our operations, resistance is negligible and easily deflected. These few individuals who are set on a course of defiance of our goals are being aggressively neutralized and eliminated.

'I will now hear the reports from our division heads.'

The meeting could have been held in any board room in any multinational corporation in the world, if not for the gruesomeness of the content. The various worldwide law enforcement groups would have drooled over the information being revealed in that room and would have certainly wished they could take advantage of being a fly on the wall.

The meeting broke up and small groups congregated as they worked their way out to their vehicles placed in select areas that allowed them to come and go without raising unwanted attention.

'What have we heard from the teams we sent out?' the leader asked his top aide. 'Anything that means we can go ahead unhindered for now?'

'The first team failed in their attempt to zero our opponents last night, but were successful in avoiding capture and identification,' the aide spoke confidently.

'The second team is preparing their strike. They intend to strike all four of the targets within twenty-four hours of team one's success against their targets. Then both teams will strike the limousine company the following night.'

'Be sure you *forcefully* remind our teams that failure is *not* an option,' the leader ordered.

15

Fred and Judy were relaxing in the student lounge between Judy's classes at the London City University.

'I'm glad that you took time off from the office,' Judy said with a sigh. 'Between quarter finals, term papers and your new responsibilities with your promotion, we barely get to say hello anymore.'

'With everything that's happened with Dad and Sally getting married, getting kidnapped and then rescued,' Fred said, nodding in agreement, 'they haven't even been able to go on their honeymoon, either. What's happening with those detectives? They seem awfully young to be the aces Capt. Reynolds claims they are.'

'They were good enough to find and rescue Mom and Mitch,' Judy reminded him. 'I feel good about them. They've shown me that they know what they're about.'

Fred shrugged his shoulders in agreement and then their conversation turned to topics of a more immediate interest. 'What do you want to do after the graduation exercises, Judy?' he asked his young wife.

'Crawl into bed and sleep for a week!' was Judy's not-so-irrelevant reply. 'I'm exhausted.'

'Too exhausted for a little playtime?' Fred pouted.

'Oh.' Judy grinned mischievously. 'I think I can conjure up some energy reserves to have some fun.'

★   ★   ★

The evening had brought a relaxing coolness after a pleasantly warm day. Mitch and Sally sat on the porch swing of Mitch's front porch.

'I think I'd like to have your porch swing out front of wherever we decide to live,' Sally remarked contentedly as they watched the sky turn a collage of colors. 'It reminds me of when I was a little girl visiting my grandparents.'

'Irene loved this old swing, too,' Mitch said. 'She was the one who insisted on buying it. Fred would climb up on the arms, hold on to the chain and pretend he was piloting a plane as he made the swing go back and forth.'

Mitch gave a sigh as he continued. 'There's a lot of good memories that go along with this swing. Even when Irene was at her sickest, she would ask me to bring her out to this swing so that she could watch the sunset or the young lovers walk by when the weather was nice enough and her pain wasn't so bad.'

'The front porch of both houses has a southern exposure,' Sally observed. 'Either house would have a similar view. As long as I had you to share that view, I could live happily in either house.'

Mitch gazed at Sally contentedly and remained silent.

*   *   *

Outside the Fair Fare Transportation offices, Sam, Jamie and R. R. discussed the questions they felt that they needed to ask Ryan Jacobs and Larry Erickson.

'One thing we need to know,' Sam pointed out, 'is who had access to Mitch and Sally's itinerary and the likely route to be taken back to their hotel. The place where they were abducted seems to be a little too convenient for my liking.'

'I don't disagree,' Jamie told them. 'Shouldn't they have taken a more traveled route to the William and Mary? After all, it is still part of the downtown area. What were they doing on a lonely back road?'

'And wouldn't they, being newlyweds, even at their ages, want to get to their room as quickly as possible after the ceremony and reception?' queried R. R.

'One would think so,' Sam reflected. 'Perhaps we should also check with the Jacksons as well. Maybe there's something else that night that no one's offered as important enough to talk about yet. Anything else either of you can think of that we would like, or need, to know?'

Jamie and R. R. both replied in the negative, and they got out of Sam's car and walked into the offices of the limo company.

May I help you?' the receptionist greeted them as they entered.

'Is Mr. Jacobs or Mr. Erickson available?' Sam said as he showed his badge and credentials wallet to her. 'We need to ask more questions about the recent car-jacking and abduction.'

The receptionist called to the back and spoke on the inter-office telephone for a few moments. 'Mr. Jacobs will be out shortly,' she said as she put down the receiver. 'Mr. Erickson has been contacted and will also on his way in soon.'

About a minute later, Jacobs invited them back to his private office. 'Erickson has been told that you wish to see him,' he said as he invited everyone to be seated. 'He's taken some time off since his beating and was just finishing breakfast at Mom and Pop's. He told me that he'd be here in about fifteen or twenty minutes.'

'That'll be fine.' Sam settled comfortably on the sofa along one wall and angled toward Jacobs's desk. 'Your vehicle was found and should be returned to you at the beginning of next week.'

'That's good news,' Jacobs responded, 'but you said that you needed to ask some questions?'

'Just a few things we'd like to clear up,' Jamie told him, 'if you don't mind, sir.'

'Whatever I can do to help, Detectives.' Jacobs swiveled his chair to face Jamie. 'They stole one of my cars, roughed up my driver and kidnapped a coupla my clients. I want 'em caught and punished!'

Sam looked quickly at R. R., sitting at the other end of the sofa, and then back at Jacobs. 'We'd like to know the itinerary and the planned route to and from the hotel,' he said, 'and who besides Erickson and yourself knew the timing and other details.'

'Just the secretary,' Jacobs replied after a short moment's thought. 'She keeps those records so's we can report the mileage and other expenses on the IRS forms. I don't believe that anyone else would know. We rotate between four drivers, and only they know the routes for their day's pick-ups and drop-offs.

'Erickson was supposed to pick up the clients at the William and Mary about half an hour before the wedding. Then, after the reception, he was to return them to their rooms. They had reservations for a plane to take 'em to their honeymoon destination for eleven the next morning. Erickson was to pick them up at ten-fifteen.'

'When did you know that they never arrived?' Jamie inquired.

'About ten forty-five,' she was answered. 'The hotel had called the kids when the Jacksons failed to check out. Their room key was still at the desk, and their luggage was still in the room and hadn't been packed. Fred and Judy Jackson called us, frantic to know if we knew if anything had happened to their parents. That's when a check of the time-out/time-in records revealed that Erickson hadn't shown up that night.'

'Jamie and I were given the case three days later,' Sam interjected. 'Any idea why it took so long?'

'No, detective.' Jacobs sounded mildly surprised. 'I reported my missing employee, clients and car as soon as I had made inquiries for myself. A detective from Missin' Persons came out and took a statement within the hour. He did say something about having to wait seventy-two hours.'

Sam looked at Jamie and saw her raise an eyebrow. *That was our first week back from medical leave* Sam told himself. *Perhaps when Capt. Reynolds heard that we were back, he decided to turn the case over to us.*

There was a knock at the door, and then Erickson walked in. 'I believe you know everybody, Larry,' Jacobs said to Erickson as he took the chair between the sofa and Jamie's chair. Erickson nodded.

'Mr. Erickson,' Jamie said, 'can you tell us why you were on the less direct route back to William and Mary's from St. Paul's Anglican Chapel? Wouldn't the newlyweds have wished to return the quickest way?'

'The GPS route planner indicated a stalled vehicle in traffic on the Queen Victoria and suggested the Thames as an alternate.'

'Why not take the Queen Anne?' Sam

asked. 'It's the closer of the north-south streets.'

'City roads was doin' routine maintenance by the time we was leavin' the church,' Erickson replied without hesitation. 'Them construction vehicles can block a lot of the road and slow traffic way down.'

R. R. unobtrusively nodded his agreement but kept quiet, deciding not make comments until he was alone with Sam and Jamie.

'Did you inform your passengers about the changes in the planned route?' Sam inquired as he took notes. Erickson nodded.

'And I asked 'em which route they wanted me to take,' Erickson answered. 'They told me to take the best way available.'

'And the route you took was the best offered by the GPS?' Jamie looked directly at the driver as she asked her question.

'So it seemed to me at the time.' His quick answer came with a steady gaze.

'Where were you when the bump-and-grab happened?' Sam spoke now, wanting to place the location of the kidnapping.

'I had just passed the King James, headed north toward Main Street,' Erickson informed him. 'A coupla street lights had burned out, so it was a bit dark.'

'And you had no reason to suspect that you were being followed?'

'No. The only car I saw had turned onto the Thames 'bout a block south of King James. After we passed the intersection, the car sorta speeded up and then bumped us at the light.'

'What happened next?' Jamie wanted to know.

'That's when the three men came up on both sides o' the limo and forced me to open the doors. They had guns out and I wasn't 'bout to argue. I told the Jacksons ta sit tight unless they was ordered outta the car.'

'What were you told to do?' Sam queried.

'I wasn't told nothin' after bein' made to unlock the doors. I was dragged outta the vehicle an' the biggest of the three hit me with his gun once or twice. Then while I was on the ground, he kicked me in the ribs real hard.'

'And the Jacksons? What happened to them?'

'From what they told me, they was pulled outta the back seat and made to wear them fancy ankle bracelets you found us bound with. They wasn't roughed up any. I guess they figured what the big guy had done to me and the guns would keep them in line 'til they had us all secured.'

'Then they put you in their car?' Jamie asked. 'What about the limo? When did they drive it away?'

'Right after I was put into the back seat. I heard the limo bein' driven off. Then I sorta blacked out.'

Erickson couldn't give any more information until the abductees had been brought to the abandoned shack just south of Rosita's. Until Sam and R. R. had rescued them, he and the Jacksons weren't sure how much time had passed since their kidnapping. They had been somewhat surprised that nearly five days had gone by.

'We was fed several times,' Erickson

141

explained when questioned. 'They never allowed us to be more than 'stomach thinks throat's been cut' hungry. We figured we was bein' fed once, mebbe twice a day. They kept the place dark as a cave all the time. They took any cell phones and watches they found on us. Wouldn't a helped much when the batteries wore down anyway. We got hungry, but the food always came before we got more'n bein' mighty uncomfortable. Mebbe like twelve hours or so.'

'Did they ever speak?' R. R. asked. 'They ever give any commands or directions?'

'No. They was quiet as a mouse in a hole surrounded by a room full of cats. They made signs or gestures, and poked and prodded when they wanted any or all of us ta do somethin'.'

'So you never heard anything that would identify them, or saw their features?' Jamie asked. 'No distinguishing marks, tattoos, or scars?'

'The only light we ever seed was from their flashlights,' Erickson responded. 'They always had the front door closed before they let us outta the back room an' placed the food on the table. When that was done, they closed the door and left. We never knew when it was day or night.'

'You had no light at all?' Sam inquired.

'We did have several long-burnin' candles,' they were told. 'We only used one at a time, not knowin' how long we'd be incarcerated. We lit a new candle from the old one that was just about burned out. We had no matches. Our kidnappers had lit the first one before they left. We figured they wouldn't be lightin' no more.'

'One more thing, Mr. Erickson,' Sam said. 'You said that they forced you to unlock the doors. How did they do that? Did they say anything?'

'The big one pointed his gun at me,' Erickson recounted, 'and he kept makin' gestures like he was unlockin' and openin' a door. He made it pretty plain what he wanted without sayin' a word.'

'Okay.' Sam got up from the sofa, followed by R. R. and Jamie. 'That'll be all for now.'

16

'It seems so strange,' Jamie remarked as they drove away. 'All of that time, and no demands were made for the Jacksons' release.'

'We know that the perps didn't intend for them to starve,' Sam replied as he manipulated the vehicle through traffic. 'They were made to feel helpless, and not in control of their destinies. They always felt threatened, but apparently were never in any immediate danger.'

'They wanted somethin',' R. R, said from the back seat. 'And they wanted them softened up good when they made their play.'

Everyone fell silent at that observation.

★ ★ ★

As Mitch and Sally continued to watch the sunset from Mitch's front porch swing, a Ford Escape drove silently by.

'Mitch,' Sally said nervously as she watched, 'let's go inside. I don't like the way that car was going by. It was like they were watching us with evil designs.'

'Are you sure you're not just spooked after having been abducted?' Mitch asked.

'Tom always said that a little paranoia was a healthy thing in his business.' She took his arm and urged him back into the house.

Without further argument, Mitch followed his bride inside his home. He had just closed the door and walked into the center of the living room as the front of the house was ripped apart by gunfire set on full automatic.

Leaping across to Sally, he pulled her, screaming, down to the floor and crawled with her to the hallway, where they had some protection from the hail of bullets and debris from the shattered window and walls.

*   *   *

Sam and his party were half a block south of Mitch Jackson's house when they heard the gunshots. Jamie grabbed the radio's microphone from its cradle and informed the dispatcher that they had heard shots fired in the vicinity of the Jackson home. She requested back-up units to that location as they proceeded to investigate what they knew that they had heard. They arrived at Mitch's house just as three men wearing ski masks were kicking in the bullet-riddled front door.

'Police!' Sam yelled after he had ordered R. R. to stay down in the back seat and jumped out of his car parked nose-first toward the men in the doorway. 'Lay down your weapons and put your hands on top of your heads. Then walk backwards toward me!'

'Do as he says,' Jamie added from her side of the car. 'Now!'

Two of the men continued into the house as the third turned and fired his weapon in Sam and Jamie's direction. They returned fire, each hitting the shooter three times, once in the head and twice in the chest. The man went down like a deflated balloon, and they cautiously advanced on the house.

R. R. had grabbed the radio mike as Sam and Jamie made a quick check of the downed shooter. 'Shots fired!' he yelled. 'Queen's Consort Avenue and Topaz Boulevard. Officers need help!'

'Who's this?' the dispatcher asked. 'What're you doing on this frequency?'

'I'm a reporter on a ride-along,' R. R. explained quickly. 'There wasn't time to drop me off after they heard the shots bein' fired. Detective Holmes and Dr. Watson found three men in ski masks breakin' down the door to the house. One man opened fire and they dropped him. They're in the house now!'

R. R. heard more gunfire. 'My God! Please send my friends help! They're outgunned!'

Having heard the shots, the dispatcher told R. R. to stay by the radio as long he was able to keep out of danger. As the dispatcher checked on the location of patrol units in the vicinity, he reported the location of the 'officers need help: shots fired' call and gave the address. Three units reported that they were less than a minute from the scene and were responding.

R. R. heard the sirens just as more gunplay erupted inside the house. The three cruisers arrived and two officers from each unit exited, shotguns and large-caliber handguns in their hands. 'You in the vehicle!' one of the officers ordered. 'Place both of your hands outside the window and identify yourself!'

'I'm a reporter for the Midnight Confessor,' he complied. 'I was on a ride-along and couldn't be dropped off after Holmes and Watson heard shots fired. When we arrived, we found the front door being kicked in. One man fired his weapon at them and shots were exchanged, while two other men continued inside.'

Just then several loud pops sounded from inside the house.

'Secure the house!' the senior patrol officer ordered. 'Two perps, two detectives, and an unknown number of civilians are inside. Don't shoot the wrong people, and don't get killed!'

The other five officers entered the house. Shouts to surrender were heard outside, and then full-auto gunfire was heard, followed by shotgun blasts. Several seconds of silence reigned before two officers, two civilians and two detectives appeared at the ruined doorway.

'The house is being secured,' one of the officers said. 'All of the perps are down and the hostages are unharmed. One officer is down with a leg wound. We need medical help, ASAP.'

17

A worried and frantic Fred and Judy Jackson met their parents at the hospital, where they were being checked for injuries and treated for shock.

'What happened?' the younger Jacksons asked in unison as they entered the examination room. 'Are you okay?'

Their worried looks relaxed as they saw that their parents were not bleeding or sporting bandages and/or slings.

'Sally felt that something wasn't right about the way the SUV drove by,' Mitch informed his son and step-daughter/daughter-in-law. 'We got back inside just before the shooting started. When it did, we took refuge in the back bedroom with the dresser shoved against the door. The detectives arrived and there was a gun battle. All three of our attackers were badly wounded and one of the responding officers was injured.'

The doctor came in and introduced

himself to Fred and Judy. 'You folks can leave whenever you wish,' he told them. 'Outside of the trauma of your ordeal, everything checks out fine. If either of you have any emotional difficulties, I would recommend some short-term counseling. Having experienced this drastic home invasion so soon after your kidnapping could be a lot to deal with without help.'

* * *

At 187 Inc., an extremely agitated leader was facing one of the other project team. 'Nothing has gone right ever since I took on this assignment!' He literally spat out the words. With saliva on his chin, he continued. 'We were asked to clean up loose ends that were thought to have been closed off more than three years ago with the death of that P. I. Now we have lost assets, unknown sources have been discovered, and there have been multiple failures by supposedly highly trained people.'

His gaze moved to the others of the team and had the three men before him longing to be anywhere but in their superior's office facing his cold fury. 'Well?' A cold, dead stare was turned on each of them. 'What have you to say for yourselves?'

'The cop pulled the reporter back through the door just as we fired,' the first man spoke up. 'The patrol car we believed we had avoided was right on our tail.'

'We had to leave the scene,' the second man said. 'We had no other choice but to disappear and try again later.'

The third man wisely decided that silence was the better part of valor.

'You are all put on notice and demoted to being team two,' the head of the murder-for-hire organization remarked without looking up from cleaning under his fingernails. 'The current team two won't survive long enough to give any information to our enemies. Now, complete your assignments without fail and don't leave evidence!'

The three turned to the exit as their boss turned his back on them in dismissal.

'Nowhere to run,' one of them said after the door closed behind them.

'Nowhere to hide,' said another.

18

Jamie looked at the two jars on the counter flanking the cash register as she and Sam walked into the establishment that just yesterday had seemed to be a home away from home.

'I don't think Johanna's gonna shake this off quickly,' Sam remarked to her as they made their way to their usual booth. 'Johanna was right last night. She has had more than her share of negative publicity recently.'

'It's not as if the department is intentionally causing her problems,' Jamie heaved a sigh. 'The criminal element has tended to become more aggressive and vengeful of late. Even the minor players act like they're Al Capone or Bugsy Malone from the prohibition era. The morgue is crowded with the results of that kind of violence.'

A familiar figure headed toward their booth and greeted them with a weary smile. 'I apologize for my tirade last night,' Johanna told them as she slid into the booth with them. 'Last night was the final plucking of a raw nerve. The front of my place has had to be replaced at least a dozen times since I bought and renovated the John Law ten years ago. It's not just the replacement costs, but the lost revenues while being closed for repairs. This place is getting a reputation as a dangerous place to hang out.'

'I know a lot of retired cops who'd hate to see you close down,' Jamie said, looking Johanna in the eye. 'Not only is this *the* place for them to keep in touch with their fellow former compatriots, but it gives them a sense of still belonging to something that they always believed to be greater than themselves, *and* you serve the best triple and quadruple chocolate concoctions anywhere in the city.'

'And that's the best endorsement any establishment could have,' agreed Sam. 'You've made rookies feel that they were contributing to something worthwhile, and not like they had to grow into the uniform before they were a part of the team and deserving of respect. You gave them confidence when they may have been doubting themselves.'

'Keep the surcharge,' Jamie suggested. 'You have to be able to keep your standards and be able to make a living for yourself and your employees. Maybe a wall of honor for the fallen of our city would help remind the public of the precepts that built this city back in the 1890s.'

'That's something to think about,' Johanna said as she got up to greet some customers that had just arrived.

★ ★ ★

Johnny Oh, a.k.a. R. R., had taken the bus to the Tenth and Jane bus stop, then walked east on Tenth to the abandoned warehouse fronting Taft. One of his informants had reported an unusual amount of activity there over the last couple of weeks.

Strolling aimlessly, he cautiously found himself a place of concealment from where he could watch the activity at the

156

warehouse. The warehouse was one of many built after WWI and renovated after 1950. Consisting of cinder blocks with a corrugated tin roof and steel support beams, it showed its age. Somehow, even though it had been closed since the end of Desert Storm, it appeared to be in excellent shape.

Having checked the real estate owner of record for the property, he had determined that the warehouse was owned by a cannery corporation, which in turn was owned by a mega-corporation with an international reach.

'Nothin's local anymore,' R. R. murmured to himself as he waited for something to happen. 'The big boys own ninety-five percent of everything that'll make 'em money or give 'em a tax write-off!'

R. R. was about to give up for the night when more than a dozen luxury SUVs, coupés and sedans began pulling into the portion of the parking lot hidden from view in the back. His long wait apparently over, he cautiously changed his position to get a better view. As he watched, men in expensive clothing, shoes, and jackets to ward off the evening's desert chill exited the vehicles accompanied by others who were obviously bodyguards.

The men and bodyguards were met at the backdoor by a large muscular man with a shaved head wearing a summer-weight leather jacket, sunglasses and highly polished shoes. He was accompanied by an equally tough-looking, severe, and well-dressed woman with raven hair cut in an ear-length bob. The two people at the door patted everyone down, making them give up any of weapons that were found or take the choice to wait outside.

'How're we to protect our principles,' one of the toughs growled, 'less'n we got our guns?'

'Not our problem,' the woman door guard replied matter-of-factly. 'We follow our orders and make sure our boss is kept safe. Anyone else is sent to the meat grinder.'

'Your a stone-cold bit — ' the man started to say.

'Don't finish that sentence,' the other

door guard said as he calmly grabbed the man by his throat and lifted him off his feet. 'We don't allow that kind of language in front of the ladies. Got it?'

Realizing the uselessness of struggling, the man eventually was able to communicate his agreement. When the door guard let the man go, the tough guy's face was very flushed and he was struggling to get his breath. He was also barely able to stand. His fellow bodyguards helped him walk into the warehouse.

The boss either commands, or buys, a lot of loyalty, R. R. mused as he watched the incident play out at the warehouse door. Deciding that he had observed as much as was safe for one night, he surreptitiously made his way west the three blocks back to the bus stop. No one appeared to be following him, so he believed himself safe as he sat down on the bench to wait for the bus.

He had just gotten comfortable when a familiar vehicle pulled up to the curb. As the window rolled down, R. R. rolled off of the bench, fell to the sidewalk, and sought cover under the bench just as two blasts from an automatic shotgun tore the back off of it. He rolled under the bench, expecting that the next blast wouldn't miss, ending his career.

Such was not to be. Two patrol cruisers with two officers in each came rushing toward the shooters, sirens blaring and lights flashing. The sedan took off, smoke rising from the squealing tires as it peeled away from the bus stop. One patrol car slowed down to allow an officer to exit the car, check on R. R., and to stay on the scene. The others were in pursuit, and one officer was giving the dispatcher a constant stream of information to be passed on to other units in the vicinity of the shooting.

The patrol officer who had stayed with R. R. quickly and efficiently interviewed him as to the events and directed the other officers who had quickly arrived in canvassing the area for witnesses. As was usual in a shooting situation, almost everyone had been too busy ducking, hiding, or fleeing to have been much help.

'This car pulled up and started

blasting,' was the usual comment with no details available.

'I thought I was gonna die!' was another regular comment.

Half an hour later, the report was made that the vehicle had been lost when it headed down an old cattle trail that led down a wide gully. 'The perps must've had four wheel drive on that sedan,' one of the pursuing officers opined. 'There was no way for us to follow them.'

Sam, Jamie and Lt. Baker arrived and had taken a shaky R. R. back to the offices of the *Midnight Confessor*. 'I guess being an investigative reporter,' Lt. Baker commented during the trip, 'is getting to be as dangerous as being a cop. Are you sure that none of those shotgun pellets or bench splinters hit you?'

'Before anythin' else,' R. R. answered, 'I want to get outta Johnny's clothes and back into R. R.'s. I'll check myself over and see if I need doctorin'. Thanks for askin'.'

'Keeping law-abiding citizens safe,' Jamie said, 'is part of our job.' *Even if their personality stinks*, she thought to herself, but didn't say out loud. *Or if their occupation is to drag folks through the mud.*

★　★　★

After R. R. had changed, he, Sam, Jamie and the lieutenant were all seated in the newspaper's conference room. R. R. gave a full account of what he had seen and was able to hear at the old warehouse. 'I think I recognized at least one civic leader and a coupla people from Maxie's mob,' he stated calmly. 'That's why I was already duckin' when the window rolled down. It was the same coupé that gave Johnny the ride to Maxie's place.'

'Now we have circumstantial evidence,' Lt. Baker observed, 'that Tom Jenkins's death was no traffic accident. Jamie, can you find out anything from the other driver's autopsy report that we may have missed from three years ago? Or anything that should have raised a red flag back then?'

'I'll have a look and see, sir,' she told the lieutenant. 'After three years, the trail will be pretty cold. Sam may not be a doctor, but he's got a good eye for detail. I'd like him to look the report over with me.'

'Then do it,' Baker ordered. 'The chief, the captain and the commissioner are all demanding a resolution to this case. I agree with them that too many bullets are flying for public safety. We've been fortunate that no innocent bystanders have been have been hurt so far.'

Baker put his jacket on as he headed toward the exit. 'This case isn't just a kidnapping anymore,' he commented as he stopped at the door. 'The opposing team is starting to play by a new set of rules. Dirty and deadly rules. Until this is over, the three of you are not to set foot inside Johanna's. You've been known to frequent the place, and that's made it too dangerous for the bystanders.'

★ ★ ★

'I can't believe we've been ordered to stay away from Johanna's.' Sam shook his head in denial later when he and Jamie were headed home. 'I've been going there ever since I inherited my parents' property and graduated from the academy. It's a second home!'

'I know exactly how you feel, Sam,' Jamie agreed. 'I didn't know anyone when I moved here after attending medical school at Johns Hopkins back east. One of the trainees from the FME department said she'd heard of a place with the best ice-cream cakes ever. So there we were, two out-of-towners made to feel that we were part of the family by the owner and the staff.'

'Maybe Johanna will let us order takeout,' Sam commented, 'and deliver it to our door.'

'That'd be nice,' said Jamie, 'but it wouldn't be the same.'

'It's still better than nothing.' Sam heaved a big, lonely sigh.

'The lieutenant made it sound as if London, CA was turning into Chicago during prohibition.' Jamie changed the subject. 'Are we becoming that dangerous, Sam?'

'I think it's as much point of view and

perception,' Sam replied after a moment's reflection. 'Yes, more shots have been fired in the last two weeks than the previous three months. Many cities of our size normally have twice that number during any two-week period. Who's to accurately claim which is more dangerous?'

'And our main job is still to protect the public and bring the 'bad people' to jail.' Jamie had a wistful smile as she spoke.

'That sounded a lot like little Jimmy.' Sam touched Jamie's arm lightly with his fingertips. 'He does see things as either black or white, good or evil, doesn't he?'

'Yes,' Jamie sighed. 'I really miss him.'

'When did you last talk to your family?' Sam asked. 'After all, you do have international minutes to the UK, you know.'

'It's been since before we were given the Jackson kidnapping case.'

'Then maybe it's time to get in touch again,' Sam suggested. 'We'll both think more clearly after we talk with your family. Does your brother have any idea how much longer his doctoral research will take?'

'He says maybe another three or four months,' Jamie told him. 'He says Jimmy's having a lot of fun with his new friends in the village. Everyone laughs and says that the other talks funny.'

'Yeah,' Sam said in thoughtful remembrance, 'he did tell me he thought the people there had silly names for things.'

'You mean like calling a television a 'telly', or the car trunk a 'boot'?' Jamie laughed at her nephew's telling her all of the strange names that he had heard familiar objects called.

'Strange enough,' Sam added, 'when you're an adult, but it must really seem strange to a three-year-old.'

19

Early the next morning, Jamie and Sam met inside Winchell's Donuts two blocks west of the City Library, ready to call Jamie's parents.

'Everyone should be back at the house by now,' Jamie said. 'It's about three in the afternoon there.'

'Wanna make a bet that Jimmy starts jumping up and down with excitement when he hears that his Aunt Jamie is calling and wants to hog the phone to tell us all about the new animals at the farms?' Sam laughed.

'No bet,' Jamie said as she punched up her contact button for her parents' phone.

The phone only rang three times before it was picked up. 'Watson's Farm,' a very young voice answered. 'Jimmy Watson speaking.'

'Well, Jimmy Watson . . . ' Jamie stifled a laugh at the grown-up tones her nephew used. ' . . . this is Jamesina Watson and Samuel Holmes calling. May we speak with your parents, or grandparents?'

Over the speaker-phone came an excited squeal and voice calling the rest of the family to come to the phone. Within moments, the sound of adult voices could be heard asking Jimmy what all of the commotion was about.

'Aunt Jamie and Sam are on the phone!' Jimmy exclaimed, his child's voice full of excitement. 'They finally called!'

Sam and Jamie heard the change in sound as the speaker-phone on the other end of the line was activated. 'Jamie, Sam,' Jamie's brother James greeted them. 'We should have known it was you. Jimmy doesn't show that kind of excitement for just anybody.'

'I'm surprised you let him answer the phone by himself,' Sam observed. 'Three years old seems kinda young for such a responsibility.'

'He's only allowed to answer the phone when one of us is in the house and we ask him to,' Jamie's dad explained. 'We're teaching telephone manners.'

'And he's very responsible for a three-year-old,' Jamie's mother added. 'After what happened with those villains when you were here, he's been very careful and obedient.'

'Anything new happening in California?' Jamie's sister-in-law Alicia asked. 'We heard you were back on active duty.'

'Captain Reynolds assigned us to a kidnapping case just to ease us back into the detective game,' Jamie told her. 'Sam and our sometime-assistant found and rescued them.'

'Were they okay?' James asked. 'Did the kidnappers give you a lot of trouble?'

'We saw them leave the old shack where they had the newlyweds and their limo driver,' Sam informed them. 'We snuck them out and returned them to their children. The chauffeur had been roughed up pretty badly, but had no permanent injuries.'

'Their children?' the Watsons in England all exclaimed together. 'They'd been married before?'

'It's too long and involved a story to

tell over the phone,' Sam explained, 'but the couple had both been widowed for some time before his son met and married her daughter.'

'A thoroughly blended family,' the eldest Watson commented.

'We think that the kidnapping of the new Mrs. Jackson may have been related to her first husband's death,' Jamie told her family.

'Like Sherlock and John,' Jamie's father ventured, 'you've stumbled into a mystery more complicated than it would first appear.'

After several minutes in which Jimmy told about going to a birthday party for one of his new friends in the village and the antics of the new puppies, everyone said goodbye, wishing that they weren't separated by so many time zones.

After another wistful ten minutes, Jamie and Sam went to the police station, where Jamie checked out the autopsy records of the second driver of the accident that killed both him and Tom Jenkins. Then she and Sam sat in her office in the FME department.

'The examiner in the case was very thorough,' Jamie observed as she read the report. 'I took the liberty of also pulling the report on Ton Jenkins, too. Maybe there'll be some relationship that wasn't recognized back then.'

'If no one was looking for it,' Sam commented, 'any relationship could have been missed. Let's see what we can find.'

For the next two hours, Jamie and Sam meticulously read each of the reports in full from the detailed reports of the examiner's observations as she opened the bodies and weighed the internal organs to the toxicology results when they had been completed. The blood work on the John Doe showed what they had been told: that the driver had a very high blood alcohol level. It also showed that a large dose of an over-the-counter cold medicine had also been taken just a short time before the accident.

Tom's autopsy report showed normal levels of all items tested except for a slightly elevated blood glucose content. 'The transcript shows that Tom's stomach had the remains of sugary food from his stop at a lunch counter just before the crash.' Jamie helped Sam interpret what he read. 'Sally told investigators that he'd sometimes get a snack on his way home if he'd missed lunch that day.'

'Did he have diabetes?' Sam inquired.

'Not that Sally knew of. His doctor said that he was in good to excellent health when he was questioned later.'

Jamie and Sam compared what they read in the autopsy reports, the accident report from the Traffic Division, and what R. R. had learned from his contacts. They each had the feeling that there was still a missing piece of the puzzle. Could the empty bottle of bourbon and the cold remedy container found in the John Doe's vehicle been enough to show up at the high levels found in his blood after such a short time between when he was observed drinking the booze and when he crashed into Tom Jenkins's car? Would it have had time to have affected his judgment and motor skills?

'The alcohol would have entered his system quickly since a check of his stomach contents showed that it was empty,' Jamie gave her medical opinion. 'Would he have been impaired enough to cause the crash accidentally? I don't know. Maybe. Could the crash have been planned by someone intent on suicide? Possibly.'

'The reports that we have from the scene showed no erratic behavior other than excessive speed until just before the driver veered into Tom's path,' Sam observed. 'Legally intoxicated or not, he was probably capable of making the decision to cause the crash. It's the 'why' that seems to be missing.'

'I think you may be right.' Jamie frowned. 'What would make someone decide to take the life of another in such a way that his own death was almost certainly assured?'

Sam was looking at the report on John Doe when a line caught his eye. 'I think we found our link between Tom's death and Sally's kidnapping,' he said excitedly. 'Read this line on tattoos, scars and skin blemishes.'

Jamie read the line that Sam was pointing to aloud. 'Left forearm, scar from possible removal of tattoo.'

'What if that tattoo had said '187' before it was removed?' Sam speculated. 'That could be the motive behind hiding a murder as a fatal accident. His investigation was getting too close to someone's illegal operations.'

Sam and Jamie took notes on their speculations and questions as they reviewed the reports before them. The pages grew in number as they noted things that put the original theories and conclusions in doubt.

'How could the original reports be so full of errors?' questioned Sam.

'Politics,' Jamie replied. 'The desire for quick solutions, and an effort to clear the case. There's not any difference between three or four years ago and today. The Powers That Be dictate their opinions and everyone else is expected to fall in line.'

'Not the best way to run a city or its police department. Let's take our questions to Sally and Judy and see what new leads we can generate.'

'And we should also ask the same questions at American Investigations,' Jamie suggested. 'A comparison of the answers should be very informative.'

'As in,' Sam responded, 'someone may not be telling everything that they know, or perhaps they may be seeing things from a different perspective.'

'Perhaps,' Jamie thought, 'we should look deeper into Fred and Mitch's activities around that time.'

'You think that they could be involved?' Sam wanted to know. 'Do you think that they may know something we're not being told?'

'I think,' Jamie said, 'that their involvement can't be discounted. Too much has happened to both families at the same time for me to believe in coincidence.'

'Instinct, based on good research and logical deduction,' Sam commented, 'is the real basis for modern detection. All of the best tools are no good unless they're used skillfully.'

Their research having taken them as far as it could for the time being, the two partners used the rest of their day to plan the order of whom they would ask first, and what questions needed to be asked of each person. They had decided to stop at the American Investigations office first, since it was the only stop that was in the eastern portion of the city. Mitch and Sally were next because both of their homes were close together in the north. Then Fred and Judy's apartment toward the southwest would be visited later if it was deemed necessary.

As they were about to leave, the report on Mitchell Jackson's mortgage had finally come in and was handed to them.

'All of the payments have been made on time or ahead of time,' Sam summarized the report for Jamie. 'He's even ahead of schedule. After the insurance paid on Irene's death and Mitch received his first retirement check, he made a substantial payment on the mortgage. It all appears in keeping with the amounts he received. Before that, the insurance paid her billable medical bills, and his paycheck paid all of the other bills. There appear to no discrepancies at first glance.'

'The purchase date on the house indicates that the house would be paid off in another six years,' Jamie observed as she looked at the purchase and pay-off dates. 'He could pay off the house in less than two years now. That would amount to a substantial savings. How much was good fortune and fortuitous financial planning and how much could be attributed to other factors? Mitch doesn't appear to be someone who would need to resort to the use of shady dealings to meet his debts, but then people do often find themselves in unexpected situations.'

'Mitch's retirement does seem to be over the top,' Sam agreed, 'even if he was employed for thirty-five years. He must have had investments in the company to have $60,000 a year in retirement benefits.'

'Something to look into,' Jamie said as they walked to her car.

20

The American Investigations building at the corner of Main Street and Taft Avenue was a building of wood, brick and mortar, and was unpretentious. 'Just about what one would expect of a prosperous house of private detectives,' Sam said as Jamie pulled into the concrete parking lot.

'They have a triple-A rating with the Better Business Bureau, too,' Jamie told Sam. 'Their satisfaction rate is 'Very Good to Excellent'. No wonder Sally's survivor's benefits were so generous. Between them and the life insurance payment, Sally had no need for government assistance to put Judy through the university.'

Sam and Jamie walked up to the door and entered the reception area. The receptionist's desk was a plain steel frame with a state-of-the-art flat screen computer monitor sitting off-center. Jamie was certain that the latest Microsoft, IBM, or Apple computer tower clone was hidden in a side drawer.

Off to the other side of the monitor was a sophisticated multi-line phone switching system. 'They must charge high rates to support all of this high-tech front-desk equipment,' Jamie said sotto voce to Sam.

'Their reputation supports their rates, I'm told,' Sam whispered back.

'We have an appointment to see your regional manager,' said Sam, holding out his badge and credentials to the receptionist. 'I'm Sgt. Holmes and this is my partner, Dr. Watson.'

'Oh, yes,' she replied with a half-smile. 'I heard of the two of you. Nice work on the super-Taser case.' Checking the computer for appointments, she told them, 'Mr. Jeffords had to step out for a moment, but he's expecting you and should return shortly. Have a seat and I'll call you as soon as he's comes in.'

After a short wait, a mature-looking gentleman in a Saks Fifth Avenue summer weight wool suit, red hair that was graying at the temples, and a stylish mustache walked in the office door. 'Have the LPD detectives arrived yet, Linda?' he asked and his secretary pointed to Sam and Jamie.

'Mr. Jeffords,' she introduced them, 'meet Sgt. Holmes and Dr. Watson. Sgt. Holmes, Dr. Watson, this is Mr. Jeffords, our regional manager.'

Jeffords offered his hand to each of his guests in a firm but non-confrontational greeting as he nodded toward the door to his office. 'Please come in and have a seat,' he invited. 'Would you care for some coffee or a soft drink?'

'No, but thanks anyway,' they both replied as they followed their host.

When everyone was seated comfortably, Sam asked, 'Were you acquainted with Tom Jenkins before his death three years ago?'

'Only by his record of closed cases.' Jeffords frowned. 'I was the district manager for San Mateo at the time. I was, of course, completely informed of the details when I became the regional manager of this area. The investigation wasn't satisfying, but the conclusions that were made were based on the evidence that we and the LPD had available at the time.'

'After the kidnapping of his widow and her new husband on their wedding night,' Jamie informed him, 'Sam and I have gathered new evidence that may challenge those conclusions. Jenkins death may well have been a murder/suicide.'

'Is this evidence something that you can share with me, Dr. Watson?' the regional manager asked. 'I know that every organization has its own rules as to when, and to whom, they will share information.'

'Some of Tom's actions just before his death may have indicated that he had concerns for his safety, and that of his family, that may have been related to a case he was working on,' Sam commented. 'From what we've been told, his last case was related to industrial espionage. Is that correct?'

'Officially.' Jeffords let out a long breath.

'And unofficially?' Jamie pushed for more information.

'He was working off the record on something that he claimed would affect a large number of prominent people in this city,' Jeffords said hesitantly. 'He was keeping what he knew to himself until he had irrefutable evidence to take before the LPD and the DA. He claimed that the people involved could afford to go all out with defamation of character, slander, and liable suits if the charges were brought up before he nailed things down.'

'Did he say anything about an organization called 187 Incorporated?' Sam inquired. 'Was there any referral to an organized death squad?'

Not that I heard of. As I said, he kept everything hush-hush and off the record. He really seemed to fear legal reprisals. From what you're telling me now, perhaps he needed to be more aware of the physical repercussions.'

'Do you have any idea where he may have kept his notes and/or theories safe until he was ready to hand them over to the DA or a trusted police official?'

'None, Sergeant.'

Sam and Jamie decided to go to the covered pavilion near the Birdhouse Fountain to compare and write up their notes. Many pieces of the puzzle were beginning to come together to make a recognizable picture. If they could find anything that Tom had written down, photographed or recorded, they could begin to build a strong enough case for the DA to take to court.

'We really need to talk with Sally and Judy,' Sam said resignedly, 'One of them *must* know where Tom might have kept records of his investigations until he was ready to turn them over to the police so that they could make an arrest, or give to his client for a civil suit.'

'Who do you want to talk to first?' Jamie asked. 'We're just about equidistant from either of them.'

'Sally is the one most likely to have the information we need,' Sam answered. 'And she's the one most apt to be available at the moment.'

The decision made, Sam called Sally's

business number. When Sally answered on the third ring, he asked if he and Jamie could drop by and talk to her about Tom's habits in keeping files on his 'work in progress' cases. She invited them to come whenever it was convenient, as she had no immediate plans and that Mitch would be busy at the Senior Center for the next couple of hours or so. It was agreed that Sam and Jamie would arrive at her home/shop within thirty minutes.

'Was she curious as to why we wanted to talk?' Jamie asked after Sam disconnected.

'She was,' Sam replied, 'but she was willing to wait when I told her that it was too sensitive for the phone lines.'

Twenty-five minutes later, Sam and Jamie pulled up in front of Sally's home and shop. The house was a single-story wood and stucco with a two-car attached garage. The garage door was open, and the half that was nearest the entrance to the house had been remodeled into a shop and sewing area. Toward the back, an old-fashioned quilting frame was set up. A framed business license was hung on the wall between the shop area and the area that reserved for parking the car that was currently in the driveway.

'Hi, Sally,' Jamie greeted her as a customer paid for a neatly folded patchwork quilt and left. 'We don't want to intrude on your business, but we are hoping that you might be able to help us.'

'Whatever I can do, Doctor.' Sally gave the two detectives a pleasant but curious look. 'I really don't know how much more I can tell you about the kidnapping.'

'What you may be able to help us with,' Sam offered, 'is some answers as to how Tom kept his records on works in progress. Did he have a special place he kept notes and things?'

'He'd sometimes put things that he was working on in a locked box in his desk here in his study. I can get the box from his desk if you'd like. When the investigators ruled his death an accident, I didn't think they needed anything that he had here at home.'

'We think perhaps,' Sam informed her, 'that he may have been working secretly on something that was more dangerous than he believed. If we could see the contents of that box, they might tell us if we are correct in our theory.'

'I'll get it for you.' Sally went into the house to retrieve the box and returned moments later. 'Here it is. Tom had the only key and it was destroyed, or lost in the accident. That was another reason I never said anything.'

'We'll be able to get it open,' Jamie said, taking the box from Sally's hands. 'The department has some expert locksmiths.'

'Please let me know if it helps you to find out why my Tom died.' Sally's face showed the unmistakable signs of unresolved questions.

'We will,' Sam promised her. 'Would Judy know of any other places that her father would have kept things while he worked on the answers to questions he may have had?'

'I don't know,' was Sally's answer. 'She might have. They were always close, and she tended to share secrets with him when she was little.'

Sam and Jamie thanked Sally for her

time and left with the lockbox. 'When does Judy finish classes today?' Jamie asked as they walked back to the car.

'Day classes are usually over by 5:00 p.m. and then the evening classes begin about 7:00 p.m.'

'Then we have enough time to grab something to eat.'

Sam and Jamie decided that the Burger King on King George and Queen Anne Avenues would be a convenient stop on the way to Fred and Judy's apartment. They could make a call from one of their cell phones to make arrangements for a meeting. The drive-thru would provide quick access to what they needed to assuage their hunger before the meeting.

'Judy should either be finished with, or between, her classes right now,' Jamie remarked, looking at her watch. 'I'll give her a call and see if she answers.'

'While you do that,' Sam said as he drove to the drive-thru order line, 'I'll put in our order.'

Jamie punched in the number to Judy's cell phone and heard the sounds of the two phones making connections. After the fourth ring, Jamie was about to disconnect when a breathless voice answered.

'Judy?' Jamie asked, not sure of the person she had reached. 'Are you all right?'

'Who's this?' she was asked in return.

'I'm Dr. Watson of the LPD. Is this Judy Jackson's phone?'

'I'm not sure who she is,' was the reply. 'The young woman collapsed outside one of the classrooms. I heard her phone ringing and thought it might be a friend or relative trying to reach her.'

'Where are you on campus?' Judy asked.

'Outside the lecture hall of the history building. The statue of the founder of the university can be seen nearby.'

'Can you stay with her until the paramedics arrive? My associate is calling them now.'

'Yes,' the Good Samaritan's voice replied. 'I think they may have been called already. Do you know if she could be pregnant? My sister fainted once or twice when she was in her early stages.'

'Since she's married,' Jamie told the voice, 'it's possible. When she regains consciousness, please let her and the paramedics know that friends are on their way. My degree is in medicine if the paramedics should ask. My partner and I should arrive in a few minutes.'

★ ★ ★

Other than being embarrassed and a little woozy, Judy was alert and in seemingly good health when Sam and Jamie arrived.

The lead paramedic was just putting away her equipment as Jamie introduced herself. 'The patient seems fine now,' she said as she offered Jamie her hand. 'Her vital signs all seem normal. This is the gentleman who stayed with her until we arrived.'

'Did you ask if Mrs. Jackson was pregnant? Our Good Samaritan wondered because she seemed to have passed out for no apparent reason.'

'That was my first question after talking to him,' the other paramedic spoke up. 'Mr. Russo is engaged to be married himself, and his sister gave birth to a boy two months ago. Mrs. Jackson claims that she and her husband haven't been *not* trying to have a baby, but she didn't know if she was for sure yet. She thought maybe.'

Jamie and Sam were introduced to Jack Russo, a young, athletic man in his mid-twenties with laughing hazel eyes and cinnamon-colored hair. 'Thanks for watching over our friend,' Sam said as he shook Jack's hand. 'The last couple of weeks have been pretty stressful, so this could have been anything. Hopefully this was because of something good happening in her life.'

Jamie told the paramedics that she and Sam would see Judy safely home, and Judy promised to make an appointment with her doctor. The campus police began to disperse the crowd and put away their report books. The excitement was over and the day's activities were returning to normal.

* * *

Jamie drove Judy home in Judy's car as Sam followed. Soon after they arrived at the apartment, Fred drove up. He had a worried look on his face as he said, 'They told me at the commons that you'd collapsed! They said the police drove you home! Are you all right? What happened?'

Judy smiled at her husband and responded, 'I just fainted, Fred. The paramedics suggested that I make an appointment with Dr. Jonas for a pregnancy test. Some women faint easily in the early months. It only means I have to be careful about how long I'm on my feet if I am.'

'You . . . me . . . ' Fred stammered and had to be helped to the couch. 'We're going to be parents?'

'She isn't sure yet, Fred,' Jamie told him with a smile. 'Let Dr. Jonas do the tests. If they're positive, *then* you can get excited, and everyone can be happy for you!'

'Now,' Sam said in a serious tone, 'to the reason Jamie and I wanted to see you, Judy. We were wondering if your dad ever left his notes on his cases with you for safekeeping. Did you have a place in your room where he might have felt them safe from unwanted scrutiny?'

After thinking for several moments, Judy answered. 'He did leave his code-book in my room not long before he died. He asked me to hold on to it for a while. After the crash, I put it in the storage locker with the things of his we wanted to keep but didn't want around to remind of us our loss. I'd all but forgotten about it.'

'What kinds of things were stored in this locker?' Jamie inquired. 'Were they mementos, records of his old cases, or what?'

'Mostly,' Judy said, 'they were notes he'd written during past cases. I felt that since Dad wouldn't be asking for it, the codebook might as well be stored in the security locker. There didn't seem to be any need for it anymore.'

21

The next day, Sam and Jamie met both Jackson families at the storage facility. The locker was a large shed of about twenty square feet with a hasp to place a personal lock on the roll-up door.

Jamie pulled out a key and walked over to the door. She hesitated a moment and then inserted the key into the lock. When the door was opened, Judy walked over to a file cabinet, took out another key and opened one of the drawers.

'Here it is,' she said as she handed a bound notebook to Sam. 'Dad kept many of his notes in code during the early stages of his investigations. Until he had the facts to back up his theories, he didn't want others to know what he'd learned. He used to say that it was a type of insurance.'

'It sounds as if your father was a prudent and cautious person,' Jamie remarked. 'In his line of work, loose lips could cause a lot of trouble.'

'Your mother gave us his lockbox that he was keeping notes from a case that he was working on but wasn't ready to report to his superiors at the time of his death,' Sam added. 'She didn't have the key. We'll have one of our locksmiths open it. We'd like you and your mother to be there when we do, and perhaps give us some insight into what he may have been thinking or working on at the time.'

'Anything to help find out what really happened.' Judy gave a sigh. 'I've always wondered if his death was an accident or something done on purpose.'

'We may only get more questions,' Sam told her, 'instead of answers.'

'I know.' Judy wiped a tear from her eye. 'But that'll be better than not knowing.'

After relocking the storage locker, everyone followed Sam's car to the locksmith's shop about a block southeast of the police station. 'Front,' a recorded voice greeted them as they walked through the door. A man with a pleasant smile that was easily seen through the grey whisker-stubble on his face walked out from the back area's workroom. As he wiped his hands on his work apron, he greeted his customers.

'Hello, Sam.' Laugh lines were visible at the corners of his eyes. 'What brings you into my shop today? Another mystery box?'

'Not this time, Daniel.' Sam pulled the lockbox out of a shopping bag and placed it on the counter. 'This box may contain the notes made by a PI about his last case before he was killed in a car accident. His widow and daughter are here to give their permission for the box to be opened and to help us understand his notes.'

'Just the right size for storing a notebook or binder,' Daniel said as he picked up the box. 'State-of-the-art keyed lock and high tensile-strength titanium. This was designed to be fireproof and virtually pick-proof.'

'Can you open it?' Jamie wondered.

'I have tools that may do the job.' Daniel looked at Sally and Judy. 'Do I have the owners' permission to bore out the lock? If the contents are flammable, they may be damaged if I have to use the torch.'

'Please do whatever you need to do,' Sally told him. 'The contents may tell us why the driver was willing to die to stop my late husband. Getting them out with as little damage as possible is the important thing.'

'I'll replace the lock and give you the keys when I'm done,' Daniel said as he took the box from the counter. 'It'd be a real shame to lose craftsmanship of this quality.'

After telling his customers that he would need at least an hour, Daniel began working on the box's lock in his workroom.

Deciding to wait in the front room, the detectives and the Jackson families relaxed on the couches and chairs, reading the magazines and sipping the coffee freshly made from the coffee-maker that Daniel provided for his customers. From the back, the whirring sound of the drill could be heard, interspersed with the sounds of light hammer blows. Finally, the noise ceased and Daniel uttered a triumphant sigh.

Daniel stepped out from behind the curtain with the box in hand and, after setting the box on the counter, he invited Sally to lift the lid. Inside was nearly an inch and half of notebook paper with neatly handwritten notes that also included precisely made drawings with numbered notations.

'I think between what we have here and Tom's codebook, we'll be much closer to what really happened to Tom Jenkins and the reason for Mitch and Sally's kidnapping,' Sam remarked as he looked at all four of the Jacksons. 'Let's find a private place inside the library where we can all look this over and see what we've got.'

* * *

In one of the library's conference rooms, Ted Jenkins's notes and codebook were spread out on the table. Sally and Jamie had sorted the notes by date and subject matter.

'Everything appears straightforward without the codebook,' Sam said, perusing the papers on the table. 'Nothing to draw

197

attention to a specific incident or circumstance.'

'That was the beauty of Tom's code to himself.' Sally sat back in her chair with a weary sigh. 'He arranged it to appear as reports on whatever he was working on, but his theories and observations were also there. Hidden in plain sight, so to speak.'

'Would the code refer to every word,' Mitch asked, 'or just to certain key words and phrases?'

'Usually just to key words and phrases,' Sally replied. 'He wasn't one to complicate matters unnecessarily.'

'We've got this room reserved for a couple of hours,' Sam informed the group. 'Why don't we break up into three teams. We can have one team read the reports out loud, another team check the codebook, and a third to write the decoded report. Things may proceed more efficiently that way.'

'Fred and I could read the reports,' Mitch volunteered, 'and take turns as our voices give out.'

'Judy and I could check the codebook

and read the translations as we find them,' Sally offered. 'We know the code better than anyone else here.'

'And Sam and I could both take down the decoded notes,' Jamie said in agreement. 'Then we could compare what we've written to see if there's anything one of us missed.'

'That sounds like a plan,' Sam commented. 'Jamie, did you bring your tape recorder? That would help keep us from missing anything.'

Jamie replied that she had her voice-activated recorder in her handbag, and brought it out. The process took nearly the full two hours, but in the end, all six people felt satisfied that they had achieved their goals.

As they packed up their belongings, Judy informed them that she would be seeing Dr. Jonas for some tests the next day. 'I had a fainting spell between classes yesterday and the paramedics suggested that I see my doctor as soon as possible,' she explained. 'They couldn't find any-thing wrong, but they felt that a check-up would be a wise move.'

'Could you be pregnant?' her mother asked carefully. 'I had a dizzy spell or two during my first trimester with you.'

'That's one of the things Dr. Jonas will be checking,' Judy replied. 'He'll also make sure that my blood sugar levels are normal. The paramedics asked me if, with all of the pressures of the end of the term, I had been eating properly.'

'Then,' Mitch chimed in with a grin, 'let's hope for the best possible answer.'

22

At the abandoned warehouse, the weed-filled parking lot had sprouted several luxury SUVs that had disgorged both well-dressed, self-important men and tough-looking gentlemen whose eyes searched the area for threats to their principles.

Inside, the leader of 187 Inc. waited behind his desk, his features hidden in the shadows. 'Thank you all for attending this emergency meeting,' he greeted his guests once they had been admitted according to his rules for being cleared for the meeting. This time there were no questions or arguments with the procedures. 'Our surveillance has revealed that our enemies may have discovered information detrimental to our enterprises. Once again, our efforts to keep our secrets have failed. Those who were to have taken care of this situation have paid the penalty. We're also looking for a traitor. This person will find himself in serious distress.'

There was murmuring and speculation among the leader's audience as they heard this news. No one wanted to be on the receiving end of the leader's tender mercies or those of his top subordinates. They each began to look for a person to blame in order to take any suspicion away from themselves.

Maxie, the leader of the Southeast organization, asked the question that was on several of the attendees' minds. 'What's happened with Johnny Oh?' he queried with a sneer on his face. 'We all know that he gathers info, then sells it to the highest bidder.'

'He's disappeared since your agents barely missed eliminating his being a problem,' Maxie was told. 'Don't you have Slash and Bash checking all of his known haunts, and informants trying to get a lead on his whereabouts? When they find him, you should be poised to take him out of the game.'

'He's been known to disappear for long periods of time, then suddenly he shows up looking to buy or sell information,' Maxie said. 'The information he buys on the street always seems to be more up to date than what he sells. Slash says that he was seen askin' about the investigator that got killed in that drunk driver accident years ago. Jerry the Rummy and Little Sawhorse were both seen talkin' to Johnny just before those cops started lookin' into the crash.'

'Find out what they said to that nosey busybody,' the leader ordered, 'then disappear everyone involved, 187 Inc.-style.'

The meeting broke up and the members of 187 Inc. stayed behind to await further orders. The trio that had guarded the door and made sure that no weapons entered the meeting room was called into the leader's sanctuary.

'This team of Holmes and Watson has been earning a reputation as a problem for business,' he told his crew. 'The Golden BBs were the first to down them after they became a team. Before that, each of them had a superb record of closing cases assigned to them. They must not be allowed to interfere with us. See that they can never again dabble in our affairs. I want their uncovering operations to be done from six feet underground from now on. Since you're now team one, make it your top priority.'

23

The gray-haired man with the military bearing had lost some of his self-assuredness as he sat alone in his private sanctuary. He peered at the information flashed on the screen of his desktop computer and scowled. His adversaries' records were disturbing.

Not only were each of them younger than one would expect with their records and levels of expertise, but each was reported to be related to persons always believed to have been fictitious. Even those ancestors known to be real had reputations for success against their enemies: there was a Watson working for MI6 during WWII, and a Holmes in intelligence endeavors in international affairs toward the end of the Korean War and during the Cold War era. Then, yet another Watson worked for the British during the Falklands War, and even another Holmes during the last days of the U.S. involvement in Vietnam.

Their families have been actively working for the established order, and to great effect, even without those fictional people in their ancestries. The leader rubbed his hand over his face and snarled aloud, 'They've come to the ends of their legacies!'

As he stood up, the light would have given one a good look at the features of his face if one had been in the room with him. The most prominent was the scar on his left cheek, the result of an old-fashioned sword duel on the field of honor. His opponent had not walked away. Von Kalter had been challenged over the affections of a young fräulein whom he had afterwards spurned, telling her that she was not worth the death of a man and that her honor was not worth defending.

After that, he had anglicized his name and moved to North America. Claiming that the scar was a fencing accident, he worked as a hired assassin, building his team of cold-blooded killers for hire. Eventually he began to call his organization after the police radio code for a suspected homicide — 187.

He had worked himself into the position of the top aide of a powerful assistant district attorney. This gave him great access to information on the people that he and his people were hired to eliminate. That was how he had first learned of Tom Jenkins and his interference in the intended corruption of the newest city official. The assistant DA, unaware of the corrupt aide in his own office, had told 'Mister Colder' that he hoped the investigator could bring him information that would lead to an arrest and conviction of the Stonewall Syndicate.

The leader had approached Stonewall with the information, and Stonewall had paid the fee to make the problem go away. Now, Jenkins's accident case was being reopened and Maxie Stonn, Stonewall's successor, was worried that what Jenkins had discovered would almost certainly bring grief to him and his people.

'Holmes and Watson wouldn't have been involved if those Jacksons had been in a traffic accident, instead of being kidnapped,' Colder's lead henchman had commented. 'These things happen all the time.'

'Traffic accidents don't always end up with the right people getting dead,' Colder reminded him. 'With the proper evidence and body-count, it would have looked as if the kidnappers had fallen out after the Jacksons and the driver had been killed. Or maybe even that a rival group tried to take over and the kidnappees were killed in the crossfire. Either way, case closed. No one left alive to tell what really happened.'

'And what about the evidence Mrs. Jackson's late first husband may have left behind?' the henchman inquired. 'Wouldn't the deaths still have caused the Jenkins case to be reopened?'

'By that time,' came the answer, 'we could have laid a false trail that would have ended in a dead end.'

★ ★ ★

Sam and Jamie were sifting through the decoded notes from Tom Jenkins' lock box at his home that evening.

'The deeper we dig into this case,' Sam commented as he stretched the kinks out of his tense muscles, 'the more it looks like Tom's death was a cover-up for murder.'

'And the more that's been uncovered,' Jamie added thoughtfully, 'the more he seems to have been on the trail of major corruption within the city government, the police department, and possibly the even the DA's office!'

'Yes,' Sam agreed, 'the assistant DA's top adjutant seems to have been implicated, along with a couple of councilmen and one of the now-retired judges. The deputy mayor's office even seems to have been tainted. If all of this had been brought to light, it would have been the worst scandal this city has ever seen. No wonder there seems to be such a massive attempt at a cover-up.'

As Sam got up to check the coffee maker, the light on his intruder alarm began flashing. Putting a finger to his lips to make Jamie aware of the need for silence, Sam retrieved his weapon from its hiding place under the upper kitchen cabinet.

Jamie pulled out her cell phone from her purse as well as her own weapon. Dialing the emergency number, she quickly and quietly let the operator know what she and Sam believed was happening outside Sam's house. The operator told her that a patrol unit was in the vicinity and was on silent approach.

'I know the officers on duty at this time of day,' Sam remarked to Jamie. 'They know that I don't jump at shadows. They'll cautiously make sure the scene is secure and let us know what they see.'

'I remember Dan and Sharon,' Jamie replied. 'Good people to have at your back.'

A soft rattle at the side entrance told Sam and Jamie that the intruders were attempting to enter the house. Sam's cell phone began vibrating, indicating an incoming text message.

'Stranger vhcle half blk from ur house,' it said. 'Back-up on way.'

Sam quickly texted back about the possible break-in attempt at his side door.

Jamie, who had been watching the doorknob, plucked at his sleeve and pointed at the door. The knob turned slowly and the door moved silently as it was slowly pushed open.

Hiding in the hallway where they could watch the door without being seen, the detectives waited until the intruders had made their way inside.

'Police!' Sam identified himself. 'Place your weapons on the floor and then put your hands on top of heads! You are officially under arrest!'

'Patrol units are outside,' Jamie told them. 'You're surrounded and cannot get away. Surrender yourselves!'

Just as it looked as though the three intruders were going to shoot it out, a voice behind them firmly said, 'Don't even try it! You'll be dead before you can even make a move.'

With that, the two men and one woman placed their weapons on the floor and interlaced their fingers on top of their heads. Dan quickly handcuffed the three suspects' hands behind their backs as Jamie, Sam and Sharon covered the three with their weapons.

'You're getting a reputation, Sam.' Sharon grinned as the suspects were placed in waiting patrol cars. 'I'm surprised the bad guys and gals would even want to try to catch you off guard in your own home.'

'When you book them,' Sam said as he returned his weapon to its hiding place, 'check them for tattoos. This may be related to a three-year-old homicide case that just might uncover a widespread corruption case.'

'We'll have them checked out before lock-up,' Dan told him. 'Any particular tattoo? Illegal entry with intent of bodily harm should hold them for a while.'

'Anything to do with 187 or 187 Inc.,' Jamie told them. 'It seems we may have a murder-for-hire cartel within the city.'

Dan and Sharon looked at each other quizzically as they returned to their car. 'Those two attract the interestingly odd the way a rotting corpse attracts flies!' Sharon remarked as she got into their unit.

★　★　★

Sam locked up his house, and then he and Jamie headed to the police station to give their statements.

'I don't believe we'll get a chance to turn in early tonight,' Jamie sighed. 'I was looking forward to a long soak in the tub and checking the weather report before getting some sleep.'

'And I was hoping to start the new historical mystery novel I found at the bookstore the other day,' Sam replied with feeling. 'It sounds interesting.'

'Not enough mysteries to solve at work?' Jamie teased.

'Every day has its own mystery, Dr. Watson,' Sam said with a straight face. 'Makes the job worth waking up to each day.'

★   ★   ★

Colder was awakened at two a.m. by the jangling of his bedside phone. 'This better be important!' he slurred in a sleepy voice. He listened for a moment and then sat up, wide awake. 'Was the team able to suicide before they could be questioned?

Why not? Okay, send out the 'scatter' signal.'

Quickly getting dressed, Colder grabbed his emergency bags and headed for the door to his hidden escape route. As he was closing it behind him, he saw the flashing red and blue lights through the curtained windows.

Now is the time that the police would start banging on the door telling me to open up if this were an old gangster movie, he thought to himself as he checked the hidden exit behind him. *Let them break down the door. I'll be out of the city by then.*

Using the decoded notes that Tom Jenkins had left behind after his death, Sam and Jamie had succeeded in getting the DA's office to awaken a friendly judge to sign several arrest warrants. The captured members of 187 Incorporated had been prevented from suicideing by lucky chance. Knowing that their lives were forfeit, and being confronted with the evidence that Tom had gathered, the three had eventually been convinced to negotiate a deal for protection by confirming what the police had already surmised. They steadfastly claimed they knew nothing more about the set-up or the operations of the 187 organization. They also claimed not to have any knowledge of the leader's identity.

'We got our orders by private messengers and P. O. box drops,' they all claimed when questioned separately.

'They're only confirming the things we already know,' Captain Reynolds said after the interrogations, 'and what they've been told we believe. Round up everyone on Jenkins's list. Bring them all in for questioning as persons of interest. Hold them as long as you can.'

As the raids were begun, no one saw the janitor hide himself in a dark corner and quietly dial a number on his cell phone.

After the janitor had made his call, he quietly and quickly left the building, disappearing into the night.

* * *

'There must have been a leak, Captain,' the squad leaders all agreed. 'More than half of the suspects were gone by the time we reached their doors.'

'Put out APBs and BOLOs on all of the missing suspects,' Lt. Baker ordered as Capt. Reynolds nodded his agreement. 'If we allow these people to go to ground, we'll never dig them out.'

The suspects who had not eluded the early-morning dragnet were being interrogated as to where a rendezvous point might be located, but to little purpose, until a councilman's intern broke down in tears. 'It was just a way of making some extra money,' she cried. 'I didn't mean any harm to anyone!'

'Were you given emergency instructions?' the female officer who was in charge of the intern's interrogation asked. 'A 'just in case' scenario?'

'Only if we were told to scatter,' she replied. 'We were told to find a place to hide. Then, after a week, we were told to go to the Aah-Aah lava beds about ten miles east of the city limits. Further instructions would be waiting at the dry creek bed.'

'Nothing more definite than that?'

'That's all. I'm not even sure I could have found it.' The young intern's eyes were dripping tears like rain. 'What's going to happen to me now? I swear that I was just running special errands for the extra money!'

'Your school tuition shouldn't have been *that* onerous,' the male police officer told her. 'What hold did they have on you?'

Weeping heavily now, the girl admitted that she had had several dates with a married man. She was told that she could stay out of trouble and protect her lover's reputation if she would give her black-mailers information on the activities of certain prominent people in the city's government and legal offices. She had no idea who the people were who had approached her, but they had shown her some very incriminating photos. These people also offered to pay her for any information she passed on to them that was of use to their needs.

'Blackmail and extortion.' The female officer shook her head as she and her partner left the young woman and the public defender in the interrogation room. 'And with payments being made for information, they've made it look as if she were a willing participant in several crimes.'

'The girl wasn't dumb,' her male partner agreed, 'just naive and unlucky.'

'Let's hope, for her sake, the DA sees it her way.'

*   *   *

Using geological survey maps, aerial photos, and road atlas maps of the area east of the city, expert topologists had finally located two or three likely places for the rendezvous.

'This spot here is where the old stagecoach line had a way station around the time the city was founded,' they told Capt. Reynolds and Lt. Baker. 'We believe that is the most likely spot. It has a dry creek bed that provides a watershed in the rainy season, ruins of enough historic interest that visitors wouldn't usually draw attention, and a lava field composed of rough basalt nearby.'

'Perhaps,' Lt. Baker suggested, 'American Investigations would be willing to help by providing some of their agents to help watch the site. After all, it was one of their agents who was killed gathering the information that got us to this point in our investigation.'

'And the chief and the commissioner would love the reduction in overtime,' the captain added. 'We'll just hide the bill from American Investigations in the discretionary funds.'

Plans for the surveillance were made after a call to American Investigations gave them the added individuals needed for proper coverage.

24

Colder had barely escaped from his house when the police forced their way through the front door. All of the visible exits had at least two officers watching for anyone leaving, but Colder's escape route was unwatched, and he reached the wooded area of the city zoo's picnic and park area.

Once he reached his exit, he quickly surveyed his surroundings. Not seeing any caretakers, park security guards or homeless persons, he proceeded cautiously down the path leading to the unguarded opening in the hedge at the corner nearest the monkey pit. Using as much stealth as he was capable of, he passed through and onto the sleep-quieted streets of the central part of the downtown area.

Seeing an all-night diner with only two or three patrons inside, he decided it would be better to find a place to hide until the early-morning crowds began to arrive. With the day-shift workers and shop owners arriving, he believed he could blend in until he could find an unsuspicious method of transportation from London to one of the larger cities west or north.

He would also need some way of disguising his scar. It made him too memorable. For now, he would hide in the men's room and apply some make-up from his stage kit. *Never leave home without it!* He looked into the diner's bathroom mirror at his as yet unshaven beard. *Perhaps a beard would change my looks just enough to get away. I'll need to dress down a bit, too.* Pulling the necessary equipment from his emergency duffel bag, Colder proceeded to change his appearance before he left the restroom.

He sat at the counter and watched the television's cable news program as the waitress took his order. 'And from eastern Riverside County,' the announcer said, 'in an unprecedented series of early-morning raids, London Police Department detectives arrested several high-ranking members and their adjutants in the city's worst corruption scandal in its history. Officials are withholding details as the investigations proceed. It's believed, however, that several highly placed aides may be members of a recently discovered murder-for-hire cartel calling itself 187 Incorporated.'

The waitress changed the channel on the TV set to a lackluster talk show before turning the set off. 'It seems there's nothin' good on before eight or nine in the morning anymore,' she said as she refilled Colder's coffee mug.

'Yeah,' he seemingly agreed. 'Used to be an insomniac could at least watch a boring rerun or a bad grade-B movie and finally fall asleep.'

★   ★   ★

The city's dragnet appeared to be more efficient than Colder had anticipated. News updates on the all-news radio stations kept increasing the numbers of arrests being made. Colder found that several of his bolt-holes were already being watched, not only by LPD people, but by men and women obviously from a large PI firm. *Must be that interfering PI firm that Jenkins worked for,* Colder mused. *They never were satisfied that his death was an accident, and now it would seem that they're out for blood!*

Looking up from his seat in the bus station, Colder saw the two people he blamed the most for the collapse of his empire, Holmes and Watson, as they searched the crowds.

'American Investigations operatives and the department both believe,' Jamie said, 'that none of the suspects have been able to leave the city. Every person that's been arrested after the initial raid has been caught trying to leave the city in some fashion.'

'The Assistant DA told us that his adjutant was a man with short gray hair, a military bearing and a recognizable scar on his left cheek,' Sam commented as they walked the streets searching for missing council people, friends of the court, suspected dirty cops, and assorted seemingly respectable felons. 'Several of these people showed up at the safe houses

Jenkins mentioned in his notes and from our captive members of 187 Inc.'

'It seems the more people we arrest, the more people are implicated,' Jamie sighed resignedly. 'It's like one of those Russian nested dolls. You know, the ones that have several dolls hidden inside each other.'

'Or like peeling an onion,' Sam replied. 'Every layer that gets removed just reveals another until there's nothing left but the odor.'

Colder turned his face away as the two detectives walked by, hoping that they wouldn't see him, or recognize him if they did. His luck held, and they were lost in the crowd as soon as they turned the corner.

The bus he was planning to take out of the city arrived. Two men in uniform were watching the passengers as they were boarding. 'Damn,' Colder said under his breath as he took in the scene. 'Where are they getting all of these people? The train stations, the taxi drivers, bus stations and drivers all seem to have people with pictures asking for ID if you even slightly resemble one of the pictures.'

Walking away from the bus and its line of boarding passengers, Colder angrily came to a decision. *No matter what happens to me,* he resolved, *I must take Holmes and Watson out, permanently!*

25

During the next forty-eight hours, it felt like half of the city's governing, legal, and enforcement personnel were either arrested or brought in for questioning. Those with direct connections to 187 Inc. nearly all fought with arresting officers, and many of them died at the scene rather than surrender. Old disputes between several factions of the city's underworld were used in the upheaval in an attempt to settle old scores under the cover of all of the arrests. London, CA was indeed looking like Chicago under thumb of prohibition racketeers. The honest, law-abiding citizens stayed off of the streets between dusk and dawn and prayed that stray bullets would not penetrate their homes.

The leader, founder, and main employer of 187 Inc. found himself trapped inside the city with seemingly no hope of escape. '*Verdammen Polizei*,' he cursed as he once more ducked into an alley to avoid patrolling police officers and PI agents deputized to augment the police not under arrest. 'Perhaps it would have been better to have moved our base of operations to a larger city instead of killing that PI. Maybe his evidence would not have been as damaging had he lived.'

A voice spoke out of the shadows. 'Psst!' it whispered. 'Want to leave the city?'

'And how would I accomplish that?' Colder asked. 'If I were looking to do so, that is.'

'Some enterprising people I know,' the hidden voice informed him, 'have a kinda underground railway. You got the where-withal to buy a ticket, we get you away from all this.'

'How much for a one-way ticket?'

'One way tickets start at $1,000,' he was told. 'The further you want go, the more it'll cost you.'

Suspecting a trap, but desperate, Colder asked, 'How far does a thousand take me?'

'Downtown Riverside,' the voice answered. 'Three thousand'll get you to the Orange County line.'

'How do I know I can trust you and your friends?' Colder inquired. 'What's to keep you from telling the cops where I'm waiting for you to pick me up after I give you my money?'

'Nothin' but a gentleman's agreement sealed with a handshake when the money changes hands.'

'And if I and your friends are caught trying to make it past the city limits?'

'Every man for himself.'

Colder and the mysterious voice made a deal to meet in an hour at a location both agreed would be safe. Colder would bring cash enough for the trip into Riverside. Recognition signals were agreed upon, and Colder heard the sound of soft-soled shoes walking away down the alley.

Colder waited until he thought the patrols had safely passed by and then made his way to the abandoned warehouse. He knew that it had already been searched and that it was probably the safest place to spend the next hour. He also believed that his hidden emergency fund was still safe. He would need it all to make good his escape.

26

At Maxie's house in the southeastern quadrant of the city, the large Amerindian was being given his orders. 'I don't care who you have to use your tactics of persuasion on, I want Johnny Oh found and brought here. We had a good thing goin' until he suddenly reappeared.' Maxie was livid. 'Hadn't been for him, a lotta our boys wouldn't be in jail without a get-outta-jail-free card. I wanna watch him get stomped on!'

The big Amerindian left with a caucasian who had a broken nose and an oriental with a slice out of his right ear. The three of them began looking in areas that Johnny was known to haunt.

'We'll try Rosita's first,' the big man told his companions. 'If we don't find him there, try a coupla the other seedy bar and grills. Then we start lookin' in alleys and the old abandoned warehouse that the leader would have us meet at.

Someone's had to have seen him. He ain't no ghost — yet.'

★   ★   ★

Colder had just entered the old ware-house when he thought he heard sirens in the distance. Quickly slipping through his secret entrance and hiding in a room whose door appeared to be a part of the wall, he felt himself secure from anyone making a search of the building. Soon he would be meeting the underground railway representative and be on his way out of the city, and then he would rebuild his organization and have his revenge on Holmes and Watson. No matter how long or how much it cost, he would see them staring lifelessly into the void. After that, he would see just how far his desire to satisfy his appetites would take him.

The time had come to make his way to the meeting that would eventually lead to his freedom and new existence. When he opened the secret door, he found three men seated in the office he had used for his meetings. Their backs were turned to the door as they watched the window for anyone approaching the warehouse.

'Time for this place to go,' he told himself. 'If Maxie thinks I'd hide here, then no place in London is safe.'

After quickly tapping a code at a digital keyboard inside the hidden room, Colder then made his way back outside and several blocks away from the warehouse. He looked back after checking his watch. 'Three, two, one,' he counted down. As he said 'zero', there was a large explosion.

'Goodbye, Maxie's goons,' he said. 'Maxie isn't the kingpin he thinks he is, and I'm not as easy to eliminate as he believes that I am.'

With a malicious smile on his face, he hurried to his meeting.

⋆   ⋆   ⋆

'One of my operatives made contact with a man we believe to be Colder,' Jeffords told Sam and Jamie as they sat in his office. 'Colder was offered a way of escaping the dragnet and they made a deal. They're to meet in about twenty minutes at the parking garage at King Henry and Jane Avenues. We'd like you two there to make the official arrest.'

'We wouldn't miss this bust for anything,' Jamie replied.

'Let's hope that this one goes better than the last time we were there,' Sam added.

'What happened?' Jeffords asked as they walked to his car.

'Two of our suspects died,' Sam answered, 'and the third got away.'

'We eventually caught him, several of his associates and his boss,' Jamie completed the scenario. 'It was a nasty case from the beginning to the end.'

When they reached Jeffords's car and got in, Sam asked, 'How many people will be in on the arrest?'

'A baker's dozen with the three of us,' Jeffords told him, and then gave Sam and Jamie the details of the plan. 'Unless he's come prepared to hunt Alaskan brown bear, we should be prepared for any eventuality.'

Famous last words, Sam and Jamie both thought.

27

The three detectives arrived at the parking garage about ten minutes before the meeting and were told that Colder was expected at the appointed time. As everyone began to take their positions, Jamie's cell phone vibrated. 'Dr. Watson,' she whispered into the receiver.

'Jamie,' Lt. Baker's voice said on the other end of the line, 'the old warehouse in the southeast quarter of town just exploded. Colder might have set it off as he left for his meeting with Jeffords's man. Be careful.'

'Do we know if anyone was in the warehouse when it exploded?' she asked.

'Not yet. Our people arrived at the scene just a few moments ago.'

'Thanks, Lieutenant. I'll pass the word along. Gotta go. I think our subject is nearly here.' Jamie clicked her phone off and quietly told Jeffords what she had heard. Jeffords nodded and got the word spread to the team.

'Do you think Maxie had people waiting at the warehouse in case Colder decided to hide out there?' Sam inquired of Jamie as they waited in their hiding place.

'I think so,' Jamie answered after a moment. 'Maxie has been mad enough to chew ten-penny nails since the raids began. Word is that Maxie has ordered Johnny Oh erased. So it's more than likely he's after Colder, too.'

The elevator was heard descending to the floor where Jeffords's team was waiting. As Colder walked out of the elevator, he was carrying a large duffel bag over his shoulder, a large-caliber automatic pistol in his right hand, and something hidden in his left.

'Are you the ticket seller?' he asked the hooded man standing by the Lincoln SUV.

The hooded man nodded his head and held out his hand for the duffel bag.

'Not all of this is for the ticket,' Colder said, reaching inside the bag and fumbling around before bringing out a large bundle of cash. '$1,000 to get me to downtown Riverside. The rest will get me someplace where I can't be traced. Now, take me to the conductor so that I can board this 'train'.'

The ticket seller gestured for Colder to follow and walked down a row of cars to an alcove where Jamie and Sam were waiting.

'I thought as much,' he said as he raised his weapon. 'No one leaves here alive. I've got enough plastic explosives connected to an idiot switch to take out this entire floor!'

'Too bad that the idiot switch has been neutralized.' Jeffords appeared from behind one of the support columns. 'As soon as you entered the garage, all electronic signals were jammed.'

'You're bluffing,' Colder said as he took his thumb away from the triggering device and dropped it.

Sam had grabbed the device and hoped that the trigger had been deactivated before the signal could get through to the bomb. Jeffords made a grab to pin Colder's arms behind his back, but before he could, Colder dropped his weapon as he dodged Jeffords, and then spun around with the bag, hitting Jeffords in the stomach and knocking the breath out of him.

As Colder raised the weapon he had just stolen from Jeffords to shoot Sam and Jamie, a dozen ruby-colored dots appeared on Colder's body as he was hit by bullets. Colder dropped to the ground, never to rise.

'Somebody please disarm the bomb!' Sam pleaded. 'The jamming device worked, but we don't know if he had a timer set up as a backup!'

One of Jeffords's men, who had been in the army's bomb squad before coming to work for American Investigations, quickly ran over to the duffel bag and began disarming the bomb. 'This was a clever set-up,' he said as he severed the last connection. 'There was a delayed trigger that would set off the bomb about a minute after it had been armed, even if the trigger hadn't been engaged.'

'Colder fully intended to die and take his enemies with him.' Jamie shook her head in disbelief. 'Fortunately, we were also well prepared for all eventualities.'

'Let's call Lt. Baker and give him our statements so we can get this case cleaned up and closed out.'

★ ★ ★

Sitting in Fred and Judy's apartment with their parents after all of the arrests had been made and all of the charges brought against the suspects, Sam and Jamie explained to everyone that everything that had happened recently had been connected to the investigations that Tom Jenkins had been secretly working on at the time of his death.

'He was a careful and thorough investigator,' Jamie told them. 'I'm certain he would have been happy that you and Mitch found each other and that Judy has found someone to share her life with.'

'He would have liked to know that he was having a grandchild,' Judy said wistfully.

'Dr. Jonas's test confirmed that?' Sam grinned at Fred and Judy.

'The baby won't be due until late summer, so she'll be able to graduate before becoming a Mom,' Fred beamed.

'Congratulations, all around!' Sam and Jamie said in unison.

⋆　⋆　⋆

Three days later, Sam's desk phone rang. It was an excited R. R. calling. Sam put him on speaker-phone so that Jamie could hear also.

'Look at the headline in the evening edition of the *Midnight Confessor!*' he told Sam and Jamie. 'This is going to win the Pulitzer Prize for sure!'

'What happened to your accent?' asked Jamie, who had been listening closely to R. R. on the speaker-phone. 'Was that a put-on?'

'Yeah, it was,' R. R. told his associates. 'But I'll bet you can't guess my real name.'

'Rumpelstiltskin!' Jamie laughed.

'Not even close, Jamie,' R. R. replied, enjoying the joke. 'It's Ronald Rogers. That's why my by-line is 'R. R'!'

We do hope that you have enjoyed reading this large print book.

Did you know that all of our titles are available for purchase?

We publish a wide range of high quality large print books including:

Romances, Mysteries, Classics
General Fiction
Non Fiction and Westerns

Special interest titles available in large print are:

The Little Oxford Dictionary
Music Book, Song Book
Hymn Book, Service Book

Also available from us courtesy of Oxford University Press:

Young Readers' Dictionary
(large print edition)
Young Readers' Thesaurus
(large print edition)

For further information or a free brochure, please contact us at:
Ulverscroft Large Print Books Ltd.,
The Green, Bradgate Road, Anstey,
Leicester, LE7 7FU, England.
Tel: (00 44) 0116 236 4325
Fax: (00 44) 0116 234 0205

THE HUNTSMAN

Gerald Verner

Superintendent Budd is faced with one of his toughest assignments in separating the strands of mystery that grip the village of Chalebury: a series of robberies perpetrated by the burglar known as Stocking-foot; sightings of the ghostly Huntsman; and the murders of a villager and a local police inspector. Interweaving with these is the suspicious behaviour of a frightened young woman who lives in a large dilapidated house with one elderly servant. Is there a connection between all these crimes and other oddities happening in the tiny village?

DREAMS IN THE NIGHT

Norman Firth

Tiring of her repressed life on a country farm, teenage beauty Alice Graham runs away from home, hoping to find a job as a journalist in New York in the Roaring Twenties. When her money runs out and she is on the edge of despair, she is befriended by Maddie, a veteran of the burlesque theatre, who takes her under her wing. But Alice soon attracts the unwelcome attentions of a New York gangster, which begins a chain of events that ignites a powder keg of murder and ultimate tragedy . . .

DEATH STALKS A LADY

Shelley Smith

After the death of her father, Judith Allen travels across the Atlantic to join the rest of her estranged family in the UK. Upon arrival, she discovers a dead woman in the garage of her mother's house, and is soon thrown into a whirlwind of adventure. As she tries to turn to her family for comfort, the people close to her start dropping like flies in mysterious circumstances. Judith is determined to follow the clues and unmask a murderer. But who can she trust?